The Cowboy Billionaire's Snowstorm

WILLOW WHITE

New Creation Publishing

Chapter 1

♥

Sunny Bodey looked out her parents' kitchen window, which, for now, was also her kitchen window. "Dad, I really don't want to go out in this."

It was March in West River, South Dakota, and it was raining. Her phone told her it was thirty-two degrees in town. She checked the thermometer on the porch, hoping that by some miracle it was a few degrees warmer at their house, but that wasn't the case.

The thermometer read thirty-one.

Her father didn't answer her, so she turned to look at him.

"Fine. I'll go," he said.

"No, no. I didn't mean that. I don't think *either* of us should go."

"Somebody has to. There's a storm coming in."

"That's what I'm saying. The storm *is* in. It's here. It's already raining. And the temperature suggests that this beautiful rain is going to freeze as soon as it hits the ground. I don't really want to drive into town on a sheet of ice." Sunny sighed. She had just filled her mother's prescription a week ago. "And you're sure we've looked everywhere for the last batch of pills?" She shifted her eyes back to her father.

"I'm sure."

Sunny didn't understand where those pills could have gone, but her mother did have a habit of misplacing things.

Her father started toward the door.

"No, no. I'll go. You stay." She had moved back home to help him with her mother. She wanted to make good on that promise. "But maybe I should keep track of the pills this time. I can dole them out to her."

"Then you're going to end up fighting with her every single day when it's time to take them."

Her mother hated taking medication. "That's okay. It's better than losing a half-full bottle of medicine." She glanced toward the living room. "I'm just going to go check on Mom real quick before I go." She walked down the narrow hallway to the other end of the house and popped her head into the room.

Her mother sat near a window, hunched over the sketch pad in her lap, her hand working furiously.

"Hey, Mom."

She didn't look up, just kept scribbling.

"I'm going into town, Mom. Do you need anything?"

"Yes, I need more yellow."

"Yeah, I'm not going to get that today. There's a storm. Do you *need* anything else?" She emphasized the word *need*.

"I *need* yellow."

Sunny forced herself to breathe. "Okay, I'll be right back. Sit tight."

Her mother finally looked up from her drawing. "Are you going to see your boyfriend?"

Sunny didn't have a boyfriend. Not even close. But her mother didn't understand how this was possible, so rather than accept that there was no one within two hundred miles for Sunny to even think about dating, her mother assumed that Sunny had a secret boyfriend. After years of battling this assumption, Sunny had resigned herself to just going along with it. It was much easier.

"I'm just running into town to get something. I'll be right back."

"Okay, tell him I said hello." She went back to her sketch. "I do wish you'd tell me who he is. I know you're embarrassed of me, but I need to meet the man you're going to marry."

Oh, for heaven's sake. No one had said anything about marriage, ever. "You will. I promise you can meet him before the wedding. And, Mom …" She wished she would look at her again, but she didn't. "Mom, I'm not embarrassed of you. Not even close."

She walked away. This last part wasn't completely accurate, but she wished it was. She tried to make it true. She loved her mother, loved her fiercely. She appreciated her for who she was and was grateful for all she'd done for her—but there *was* a small amount of embarrassment lurking down in the depths of Sunny's psyche. She wished it wasn't there, but she didn't know how to root it out.

Her father hadn't moved from his spot by the fridge.

"All right, I'm really leaving." She rested her hand on the doorknob.

"You'll be fine. You know how to drive in bad weather."

She put her coat on and pulled her hood up.

"Hey, Sun?"

She turned back.

"I sure do love you."

"I know, Dad. Thanks."

"And I appreciate all you do for us." He sounded tired.

"I know." Part of her wanted to cross the room and give him a big hug, but most of her wanted to get this over with. "I'll be right back, and then we'll hunker down."

He smiled. "Okay, sweetie."

She stepped outside and started toward the car. The wind and rain made her want to hurry, but she didn't want to slip, so she concentrated on keeping her feet under her.

Finally, she made it to her car. She slammed the door behind her, started the engine, rubbed her hands together, and muttered a quick prayer. She was five miles from the pharmacy. A piece of cake when the heavens weren't dumping rain onto the freezing earth. She put the car in gear and started up her driveway. The house was built in a small hollow, so it was a slight incline up to the road. Normally, no one even noticed it. Now it might as well have been a sheer rock face of Mount Everest. She chuckled. She had no idea what Mount Everest looked like. She had no idea what anything looked like. Despite spending her whole life dreaming of traveling the world, she'd never gone anywhere ever.

It was all South Dakota all the time.

Slowly, her car crept toward the road. Maybe the ground was warmer than she thought. There didn't seem to be any ice. Yet. She pulled out onto the road. Still all good. She exhaled slowly and fully. This was okay. She was going to be okay. Get to the drugstore, get the medication, get home, and burrow in.

She was going to make macaroni and cheese, and all was going to be right with the world.

Fortunately for her, she was warming up to South Dakota. She'd hated it as a teen, but it was growing on her. It did have its perks. The people were kind, and the landscape was beautiful. She had her best friend Brooke back.

Oh. She should probably check in with that best friend. She was going right by the Bannon Ranch, and she knew Brooke wasn't feeling well. What was one extra driveway when she had to go ten miles anyway? Besides, if anyone had the manpower and the money to keep their driveway salted, it was the Bannons.

She told her phone to open its text app. Then she told it to text Brooke. "Going to pharmacy. Do you need anything?"

Brooke had a whole house full of people ready and willing to wait on her, but sometimes a woman needed things she didn't want to ask a bunch of men for. Or a mother-in-law for.

Sunny's phone rang. She hit the button on her steering wheel to answer it.

"Sorry," Brooke said. "I thought it would be too hard to text what I'm trying to say."

Sunny could hear the sickness in her voice. "Oh no. It's not better?"

Brooke laughed bitterly. "It's so not better. It's worse. I swear, if I'd known it was going to feel like this, I really wouldn't have gotten pregnant."

"It'll be worth it." She had no idea if this were true, but it's what everyone said. "I promise."

"Anyway, I don't need anything really, but I know you know all about the hippie all-natural remedies for everything, and I didn't know if you knew of anything that might help. This is getting beyond old. I can't keep anything down. I'm concerned about dehydration. Pretty sure this baby inside me needs some hydration, you know, to *grow*."

Sunny chuckled. "Yeah. I know a few tricks."

Brooke sighed. "Good. Thank you. Don't make any special stops. If the Apothecary Shop doesn't have what you're thinking of, I can wait till after the storm."

"I think they'll have something helpful. Until then, there must be some form of peppermint in that mansion."

"It's not a mansion, and peppermint?"

"Yeah, it sounds too simple to work, but it does. But it has to be real peppermint. So peppermint tea, or mints, or oil–"

"You want me to drink peppermint oil?"

"No!" Goodness, good thing she'd asked for clarification. "Are you mad? You just rub it on your tummy and sniff it."

"Sniff my tummy?"

Sunny groaned. "Sniff the oil however you want. Before, after, or while it's on your tummy. Maybe you should just stick to the tea. I'm going to hang up now. These roads are making me nervous. I need to focus."

"It's bad?"

"Not yet, but it's raining, the wind is blowing my car around, and it's below freezing, so it's not good."

"Okay, be safe, my friend. Thanks for thinking of me. I'll ask Callum to make sure the driveway is salted."

"You bet. See you in a few." Sunny hung up the phone and gave it as much gas as she dared. She was in a hurry to get this mission over with.

There was a piping hot bowl of mac and cheese in her future, and she wanted to get home to it.

Chapter 2

Patrick Bannon came in out of the rain and took off his hat. He shook the water off it and hung it by the door, alongside the many other hats owned by the many men currently living in his brother Callum's house.

Patrick had grown up in this house, and it still felt like home, but it was also obvious that things had changed. Callum had gotten married, he had two teen sons running around, and his wife was pregnant.

That didn't leave a lot of room for Patrick. In terms of feet and inches, there was plenty of space. The house was large, and there were still bedrooms to spare. But emotionally, it was crowded. He was a grown man, used to living on the other side of the world. It was weird now to be a guest in his brother's house, no matter how much his mother told him that it wasn't weird.

"You're only visiting. So relax. Let us treat you like an honored guest." Ma had said some variation of this at least ten times.

But the thing was, the thing he hadn't yet told his mother, was that he wasn't sure how long he was staying. Maybe he wasn't just visiting this time. Maybe it was time to stay put.

Officially, he'd come home for his brother Liam's wedding—which wasn't supposed to happen for another two months.

Patrick was a smidgen early.

He'd told his family he was on vacation. He'd told his agency he was on respite.

He didn't know what he was on. He only knew that he was exhausted. But this—this rattling around aimlessly in his brother's house wasn't what he needed either. For more than a decade he'd been working all day every day as hard as he could.

Now that he genuinely wanted to relax, *needed* to relax, he couldn't quite make himself do it. How could resting be so hard? He didn't know, but it was. He ambled toward the kitchen. His mother's cooking fixed most problems, and it was just about lunchtime.

She greeted him with an excited hug. "Ah! It's so good to see you!"

"Ma, I've been here for two days."

She gave him a stern look. "And it's going to be a lot more days before I stop getting excited to see you."

Callum came into the room. "You're never that excited to see me, Ma. You're going to give me a complex."

She narrowed her eyes and waggled a scolding finger at him. "How is your wife feeling?"

"Terrible." Callum sat. "I'll take her up a plate of food, but I don't think she'll eat it." His phone beeped, and he pulled it out of his pocket.

"You don't need that thing at the table. I don't care how big a businessman you are."

Callum groaned. "It's my wife, Ma. She's asking for peppermint tea." He looked up. "Do you have any?"

"Peppermint tea?" She looked offended. "Of course I have peppermint tea. Coming right up."

"Thanks, Ma."

Callum's boys came in then, followed by their aunt.

"What's for lunch?" Deedee asked.

Ma looked up. "Sweetie! I didn't even know you were here."

"I just got here. Figured we might lose power and wanted to be where there was a generator."

"I don't know why you don't just live here," Patrick said. "If not in this house, then somewhere on the ranch."

"I don't know why *you* don't just live here," she shot back at him. "At least I don't live in West Africa."

He grinned. She had a point.

"I like it in town," Deedee said. "There's more going on."

"And yet you're always here," Callum said.

"I like it here too." She sat and then scooted her chair closer to the table. "That's why I don't live here. This way, I get the best of both worlds."

Ma set two roasted chickens in the middle of the table. "I think you've got a pretty good arrangement." She made her way to the head of the table and then nodded to Callum. "Would you say ..." She stopped herself. "You know what? Would you mind if Patrick said grace today?" She smiled at him. "Yes, I think that would be nice."

Patrick didn't mind saying grace, but he hoped his mother didn't think his prayer would carry some extra power because he was a missionary. That wasn't how it worked.

Callum waved at him. "By all means, go for it."

Patrick took a big breath and then bowed his head. He said grace without thinking about the words and then said amen. When he picked up his head, his mother was looking right at him, and there was concern in her eyes. He tried to appear strong, but he felt exposed under her gaze, and he averted his eyes. He didn't need his mother knowing that all was not as it should be in his heart. If she hugged him and told him to come home, he might crumble into a little kid version of himself, and that would not be good. He wasn't a little kid anymore. He was a grown man, and he needed to act like it. He needed to solve his own problems. He needed to get his heart right.

He sighed and focused on his lunch, which was delicious. He didn't know how to get his heart right when he didn't really know what was wrong with it. He was just so tired. His missionary mentor had told him that he was flirting with burn out and that he needed to get some rest before that happened, but rest didn't seem to be helping. Yes, his last few months in Africa had been long days of constant exhaustion, but now that he was here, supposedly resting, all he felt was guilt, not rejuvenation, not recovery, not excitement to go back.

Only guilt.

There was so much there waiting for him. So many people hurting. So many people who needed God's love.

"This is really good, Ma. Thank you."

"My pleasure. Have some more green beans. They're from my garden."

David looked perplexed. "What garden? It's frozen."

Her face fell. Patrick could read her mind. She was thinking that her two grandsons had spent too much of their youth in a city. "We preserve our bounty and enjoy it all year long," Ma said.

"Oh." David took a bite of bread, obviously having lost interest.

"You saw Brooke and me in here with a hundred jars," Ma continued. "What did you think we were doing?"

He didn't answer her.

"I would love some more green beans." Patrick held his plate out in an attempt to rescue his nephew, who gave him a grateful look.

Patrick smiled at him. That was another reason to stick around here. His nephews were home. He hadn't known them since they were little. He would like to know them now, and there was another one on the way. Then he thought of all the little kids in Africa, the kids he genuinely loved, the kids who adored him, and his heart was torn. How had he ended up like this, with a piece of his soul on two different continents?

He finished his meal before the others were done and got up to start the dishes.

"Don't worry about that, Patrick," Ma said. "I'll get them."

He didn't understand why, with all the wealth his mother had, she didn't hire help for such tasks, but he also admired her for it. She might be rich, but she was still just a God-fearing rancher's wife. Well, a rancher's widow now. "Let me help, Ma. I want to do it. You did my dishes for the first sixteen years of my life."

She laughed, and it was a cute, squeaky laugh. "Are you suggesting that you started doing dishes when you were sixteen?"

That was the way he remembered it. "Yeah. At least some of the time."

"Oh my." She gasped and put the back of her hand to her forehead. "I must be getting forgetful in my old age. I don't remember it that way at all!"

He let her have her drama and started scrubbing instead of arguing. Before long, he was lost in a blissful sort of trance. His family members were happy to pile onto his workload, and he was happy to have his hands in hot running water while the cold rain pinged off the window in front of him. The chatter of voices around the table melded into one sweet, even if discordant, song that made his heart warm. This was nice.

By the time he'd finished the dishes, Ma was the only one left in the kitchen. She had already dried and put away half the dishes when he picked up a towel to help her finish. His eyes fell on the top-of-the-line dishwasher. "Do you ever use that?"

She smiled. "About half the time. Sometimes I forget it's there. Usually we have such a big crowd that the dishes don't all fit in it anyway."

This didn't surprise him. "I bet Callum could find you a bigger one. Or put two side by side."

She waved him off and grabbed another dish. "Nah, I'm fine without it. Though one day Brooke will be taking over, and maybe she'll want an extra dishwasher."

Patrick smirked at her. "You're such a sexist, Ma. How do you know Callum won't be the one doing the dishes?"

She barked out a laugh. "Hardly! That man would rather starve than have to clean a plate to eat off."

Patrick chuckled. "I don't think it's his aversion to plate-washing. I think he just gets so busy he forgets to eat."

"Yes," she said contemplatively. "I suppose that's true. But he still doesn't like to do dishes."

"He might be working too hard. He reminds me of Dad." Patrick could feel her winding up to dive into his personal life, so he wanted to shift the attention to a brother if he could.

It didn't work. She leaned on the counter. "Are you doing okay, honey?"

"Yes, of course. Why wouldn't I be?" That was a good question.

"You just seem ... not yourself."

He sighed. "I'm just tired."

"I can't imagine your life," she said softly. "You've been doing this a long time, Patrick."

He didn't know what to say to that.

"You know ..." She chuckled thoughtfully. "I used to worry myself sick when you first started talking about going into missions and then when you actually went. I was worried about malaria and poisonous snakes and civil wars, but now ... now I think there might be a bigger threat than any of those things."

He looked at her, surprised. "What?"

She shook her head. "I'm not really sure. I don't know what it is or what to call it. You call it tired. I guess that's as good a word as any, but one can be tired, take a nap, and jump right up, or one can be *tired* ..."

Again, he didn't know what to say.

"How much time does a single man usually spend in the field?"

He shrugged. "It varies. Some spend their whole lives—"

"And the others?"

He shifted his weight to his other foot. "I don't know." He let out a long breath. "I've heard twelve years."

"And haven't I heard that a lot of missionaries don't even fulfill their first commitment and come home early?" Her voice did not hold an ounce of criticism. There was only concern and compassion. She would have made a great missionary herself.

"Yes, but that's usually due to lack of funding, and that's never been my problem."

"You know," she said softly, "if you decide to move on to the next chapter of your life, we could still keep supporting the mission." She paused. "We could send money to some young blood with some young energy." She smiled. "Like you used to have."

"You make it sound like I'm so old."

"Not old, honey. Just grown up."

He heard voices in the foyer.

"Seems we have company," Ma said.

"In this?" Patrick looked out the window. "It's probably just a ranch hand." But he could clearly hear a woman's voice, and it didn't sound like Blade.

Ma looked out the window too. "That looks like Sunny's truck."

His breath hitched at the sound of her name.

"She's probably here to visit Brooke," Ma continued.

Patrick glanced outside. "In this?" he said again.

Ma headed toward the door. "I don't think Sunny Bodey is big on common sense."

Patrick followed his mother, annoyed at the nerves tickling his stomach. He had endured a monster crush on Sunny when they were in high school. Then he hadn't seen her in years. But when he saw her at Shane's wedding, he'd nearly keeled over from her beauty. He hadn't managed to get up the nerve to talk to her then. Maybe this was his chance.

There she was, dripping in the foyer. And it looked like she was about to leave. Maybe this wasn't his chance.

"Do you want to stay, Sunny?" Ma asked. "You could wait out the storm here."

Patrick considered crossing his fingers.

"Thank you, but I've got to get back to Mom." She nodded toward Callum, who held a small, damp paper bag. "I was just dropping off some herbs for Brooke." She smiled at Ma and then at him, and he felt that smile like a physical force. "I'll get out of your hair." And then she was gone, back out into the storm like a complete nut.

He stepped to the window and watched her walk to her car, climb in, and then drive away. What a bummer. He almost laughed at himself. He was verging on pathetic.

It was too early to go to bed, so he went into the living room to find something on TV. When he was in the States, he tried to catch up on as much TV as possible. He knew it rotted his brain, but it was just so fun and entertaining that he allowed himself to binge while he could.

Callum and the boys were already in there, watching *Hawkeye*. He settled into a recliner and joined the party.

Only a few minutes later, Brooke came into the room looking even more exhausted then he felt. At least he didn't have to be pregnant.

"Honey?" she said to Callum.

The concern in her voice made Patrick sit up straight.

"Sunny just called. She's gone off the road. Can you go get her?"

"I'll go!" Patrick jumped up so fast that Callum looked at him suspiciously. "You stay here with your family," he said quickly, awkwardly. "I'll go. I'm bored." This was a white lie, but it was too late to reel it back in. "Did she say where she was?" he asked on his way to the door.

Brooke followed him. "No, but she's between here and her house, so that's not much territory."

"Where's her house?"

Brooke rattled off the address.

He nodded and put his hat on. "Got it."

"You know where that is?"

He nodded again. "There are only seven roads in West Hope. I'll find her." And then he was out in the cold rain. The wind hit him like a moving wall, and he braced himself against it. It was miserable out, but he was glad to be doing what he was doing. He was excited to see Sunny again, and it felt good to have a mission.

Chapter 3

♥

Sunny reclined her seat and bit her lip. She was so angry at herself. Really? She couldn't manage the few miles to her house? She had to go and drive into the ditch? Luckily, it was a shallow ditch, not really much of a ditch at all in fact, but enough of a ditch to have her stuck in it. Her front tires just spun helplessly when she tried to back out of it. There were no people in sight. There was nothing in sight except ice and freezing rain. At least her car was running, so she wouldn't freeze to death. And Brooke was sending Callum, who would be there any minute, and she would be rescued. The only thing injured here was her pride, and that would recover. Probably.

But the minutes ticked by, and no Callum.

Trying not to be nervous, she kept glancing at her fuel gauge, where the needle hovered over the capital E. How many times in her life had her father told her not to drive around on empty? Especially in South Dakota, especially in the winter.

Several hundred, at least.

But gas was expensive.

It's not that she couldn't afford to put gas in her tank. She could. She had a job and didn't have many bills. There were just so many better things to spend money on than gas. And so, she never filled up unless she was going on a road trip. Instead, she would squirt a few dollars at a time into her tank—just enough to get her to work and back.

She let out a long sigh. She had enough gas. As long as Callum got there soon. Where was he? Had he gone off the road too? Even his fancy gazillion-dollar pickup truck didn't guarantee safety with ice. She glanced at her phone. She definitely wasn't calling Callum. That would be weird. But she could call Brooke and ask her to call Callum? Maybe ask how much longer? But then Brooke might get scared. It was bad enough that her best friend was in bed trying not to throw up her tea. Sunny didn't want to add fear over her husband's safety to the mix.

She wished she was better friends with one of the Bannons. She could text Deedee or Finn or ... She remembered the way Patrick had looked at her when she'd dropped off the herbs. What had that been about? He'd made bona fide googly eyes at her.

Once, years ago, she'd gotten really dressed up to go to a poetry reading in Rapid City. She'd been trying to impress a poet named August—that man had been so gorgeous—and she'd gotten all decked out. Big hair, big dress, big makeup ... she'd even gotten her nails done. Looking like a million bucks, she'd had to pee, and she'd stopped at Family Fare to take care of business. Worried she was going to be late to the reading, she'd asked a Family Fare worker if he could point her toward the restroom, and the question had struck him dumb. He stood there staring at her as if he was starstruck. She'd had to find the restroom without his help.

No one had looked at her like that since.

Until Patrick Bannon.

But she certainly wasn't decked out to the nines today. She hadn't showered, her hair was in a rat's-nest-bun on top of her head, and she was wrapped in a stained winter coat.

It didn't make sense.

Sure, Patrick hadn't seen her in a while. Maybe he was just reacting to how much she'd changed. But wait, he had seen her at Shane's wedding. She tried to remember back. Had he looked at her funny then? She couldn't remember. She didn't think she'd ever gotten close to him.

She shook her head to clear it. She didn't need to be meditating on Patrick Bannon. She checked her phone. Two minutes had gone by since she'd last checked. Good. She hadn't been meditating on Patrick too long then. She checked the gas gauge again.

Maybe she should turn the engine off to save her gas. She could start it again if she got cold. She didn't like this idea. She knew she wouldn't freeze to death if she turned her car off for ten minutes, but the running engine felt like a security blanket. Still, it would be wise to give the gas a break. She put her hand on the key—wait. Would it take more gas to start the car again than it would to let it idle? She leaned back and let her hand drop. She didn't know.

She picked up her phone to ask the world wide web that question.

Chapter 4

Patrick peered into the rain. Despite the heroic effort of his windshield wipers, it was nearly impossible to see anything.

He'd already driven all the way to Sunny's parents' house, figured he'd missed her, and then, feeling quite foolish, turned around to head back toward his family's ranch, going much slower this time. But he was almost back to the house, and—no Sunny.

He picked up his phone and called Callum, who answered on the first ring.

"Hey," Patrick said. "I can't find her."

"You can't find her?" He sounded incredulous.

"Yeah. I know it's weird. Can you check with Brooke, make sure she was headed back to her parents' house? Or make sure I've got the right address?" He repeated it.

"Yeah, sure. I'll call her."

"Call her?" Couldn't he just go upstairs and ask?

"Yeah, I'm in the barn. Call you right back."

"Hey, wait!"

"Yeah?"

"Can you ask Brooke to text me Sunny's number?"

"Yeah, sure."

Patrick hung up and let the phone drop to his lap as his eyes continued to scan both sides of the road. There were no other vehicles on the road. He was the only one dumb or desperate enough to be out in this. Well, he and Sunny.

A mile later, Callum called back. "Brooke says she takes Red Bird Road."

"What?" He knew what Red Bird Road was, but that didn't make any sense. Why would she take a back road in an ice storm?

Callum didn't answer. He knew that Patrick knew what Red Bird Road was.

"Why would she do that?" Patrick asked.

"I don't know, brother. Sunny does weird things."

"Okay. I'll head that way." He sped up so he could quickly find a place to turn around but then slowed again when his tires skittered sideways beneath him. Sunny had been wearing a thick winter coat and good boots. She would be okay. Besides, she was probably still snuggled up in her nice warm car.

His phone chirped, letting him know he had a text message. He waited until he was stopped at the foot of his driveway to look at it. All it contained was a South Dakota phone number. Sunny's phone number.

Butterflies attacked his stomach. Well, that was stupid. If the woman was caught out in a storm, he didn't need to be nervous about calling her. But he still was. It felt presumptuous. So he quickly wrote her a text instead. "Brooke said you're on Red Bird. On my way." He pressed send. If she wasn't on Red Bird, she would correct him, right?

He turned the truck around and headed north again, still looking for her car even though it had been determined that she wouldn't be on this road.

He slowed and carefully made the turn onto Red Bird. Why on earth would she have taken this road? He didn't think it was a shortcut in good weather, let alone in this. Did the trucks even sand this road? This woman was either crazy, or she really liked adventure.

His phone chirped again. He didn't have his phone hooked up to the truck's Bluetooth, and he didn't want to take his eyes off the road, so he ignored it. He could check it when he found her or when he got to the end of Red Bird, whichever came first.

Finally, a grayish profile emerged out of the blurry scene in front of him. Yes, that was definitely a car, and it didn't appear to be on the road. Breath rushed out of him, and his shoulders relaxed. He hadn't realized how worried he'd been about her. The scene grew clearer as he drew nearer. Yes, that was definitely her. His relief gave way to excitement. He was grateful to be her hero, even if it was just for a minute, and even if she wasn't truly in any grave danger.

He started tapping the brakes long before he reached her, thinking he might not be able to stop at all. But the tires found traction. Good old Callum. Patrick made fun of him for his obsession with having the best trucks, the best parts, the best tires, but right now his obsession seemed objectively necessary. He came to a stop and rolled down his window, but she was already getting out of the car and wasn't looking his way, so he promptly rolled the window back up to block the sharp blades of rain that were blowing into his face.

He looked down at his phone. It was a text from Sunny. "Yes, I'm on Red Road. Thanks, Callum."

She was expecting Callum. That made sense. Patrick hoped she wouldn't be disappointed.

Chapter 5

♥

S unny ripped the Bannon Ranch truck's door open and threw herself inside. She hurried to shut the door behind her and then closed her eyes. What sweet relief. Her car had been warm enough, but this felt much warmer. It felt safe. It even *smelled* safe. She wondered if this was what Noah felt like when he was safely tucked into the ark. Probably not quite. The ark probably didn't smell like leather and Armor All.

She opened her eyes to look at Callum and then startled. "Hey!" she cried with more surprise than was reasonable.

Patrick Bannon grinned broadly. "Hey, yourself. Sorry, I know you were expecting Callum."

"No, no," she said, too quickly. "That's cool. Thanks so much for coming." She hurried to look away from him, using her seatbelt as an excuse. She fumbled with it, though, and felt even more foolish. Finally, she got it snapped into place, and Patrick started driving.

She tried to relax. This wasn't a big deal. He wasn't even making googly eyes at her. That could have easily been all in her head.

"Not to be critical," he said, and she braced herself. No sentence that started like that ended up not being critical. "But why did you take this road?"

"It's a shortcut." In her peripheral vision, she saw him turn toward her. She didn't meet his eyes, but when he kept staring, she finally turned to look at him, mostly because she wanted his eyes on the road.

He was smiling, and, true to his word, there wasn't an ounce of criticism in those eyes. There was something else. Not quite googly eyes, but definitely a spark. She dropped her eyes. That gaze was making her insides all squishy and confusing. "You should watch the road."

He chuckled softly. "I'm not sure this road is a shortcut on the driest, sunniest day in July."

"It is," she said quickly. "I've measured it."

He laughed again. "What? Why?"

"I don't know. I like to save gas. I figure out the shortest way to get to everywhere."

"There is no short way to get anywhere when you live out here."

She laughed, and the laughter relaxed her. "Ain't that the truth." She leaned back into the leather. She was excited to get home, but part of her didn't want to get out of this truck. She tried to savor the moment.

"How are your folks?" he asked.

"Good." She could feel his eyes on her again, but this time she didn't take the bait. If he wanted to drive into the ditch, they could call Callum.

"Good," he finally said. "Brooke said you had to go to the drugstore for them, so I was worried someone was sick."

"No. Not sick. My mom just has ... issues." A lot of people knew about her mother, but she wasn't sure Patrick did. Did the Bannons pay attention to local scuttlebutt? They might be above it. Her high school friends had certainly known about her mother, but Patrick had been a few years ahead of her in school. She remembered him then, suddenly, brightly, in color. He had been such a goofy looking kid. Tall and lanky, all ears and freckles and bright red hair. She sneaked a peek at him. He wasn't goofy looking now. Not at all. He was muscular with a strong jaw line and full lips—she yanked her eyes front. Why on earth was she looking at Patrick Bannon's *lips*? She had to get a grip!

"Well, she's an artist, right? Aren't all artists a little eccentric?"

She looked at him again. She couldn't help herself. Either he had no idea the extent of her mother's *eccentricity* or he was being kind. "I guess I don't know. I only know one artist, really." Her mother had enjoyed a plethora of artist friends when Sunny was little, but that was a long time ago.

"It makes sense. They see the world through different eyes. I would imagine they get a lot more ... I'm not sure how to say it. Data, maybe? Input? You know, they take in more information so that they can process it, condense it, and create their version of it."

She knew she was staring at him, but she couldn't help it.

He glanced at her and then immediately back to the road. "Or something like that," he said, sounding self-conscious.

"No, I think it's exactly like that. I've just never heard it put quite that way. Oh my stars"—she finally managed to pull her eyes away from his profile— "my mother would *love* you."

He chuckled. "Most do," he said quietly. Then just as she was realizing the weirdness of that comment, he hurried to clarify. "I work with a lot of kids, and I am pretty good with them, so their mothers like me. Usually. Sorry. Didn't mean to sound creepy."

She giggled softly. "Not creepy at all." An image flashed through her brain. Patrick in an African jungle with a swarm of children around him. Of course they would love him. "Do you wear your cowboy hat in Africa?"

He belted out a laugh. "What? No."

Her cheeks got hot. Why had she asked that? "Sorry. I was just picturing you there and wanted to make sure my picture was accurate."

Chapter 6

♥

Patrick knew he was driving at the speed of molasses flow, but he was so happy he didn't want to ever arrive at Sunny's house. Besides, if anyone called him out on it, he could just say he was erring on the side of safety.

She was picturing him in Africa? That was pretty cool. *Easy there, bud. Don't get too excited.* Even if she found him interesting, he still had to go back to Africa. He doubted Sunny Bodey would want to move to Africa.

"It's so cool that you live in Africa."

Or maybe she would.

"Pretty hot actually."

She didn't laugh.

"Sorry. Lame joke."

"No, it wasn't. I was just thinking about it. Such a different culture. I would love to visit." She sounded wistful. "Although, I'd love to visit just about anywhere."

"Oh yeah?" He wanted to keep her talking. Not only was she interesting, but he liked the sound of her voice. And their little impromptu date was going to be over soon.

"Yeah." She sighed. "I've always wanted to travel. And I mean, I will, one day. But my list of destinations is about a mile long, so I would never be able to see them all." She gave him a sweet smile. "And I'll admit, West Africa isn't at the tippy top of my list."

"No? What is?"

"You know what?" She sounded contemplative. "It would be pretty close to the top now that I think about it. But the tippy top, I suppose, would be Paris. And then there's more mundane places that I'd really like to see. New York City. Alaska."

He laughed. "Quite the variety there."

She giggled. "Variety is the spice of life."

"And I don't think New York City is mundane."

"No, I know that. But it's not as exotic as Paris. Mundane isn't the right word. I don't know what I'm trying to say. You ever been there?"

"What? To New York City?" He'd rather saw off a foot.

"Yeah."

"No, can't say that I have."

"Well, after Paris, that's probably my second stop. All those people bustling about. All those shows to see. I could save for years and only see one Broadway show, but it would be worth it."

An idea sprang into his mind, and he had to use incredible self-control not to blurt it out. He tried to sound cool. "Liam and Blade love the opera house in Homestake. Have you ever been?" His stomach felt like a butterfly house. *Play it cool. It's only a date.*

She snorted derisively. "Yes, and that's not Broadway."

Okay, then, so not a date at all. The end of her parents' driveway came into view. Should he ask her out? No. Maybe he should. Maybe not. His brain felt like a popcorn machine. "What do you want to do in Paris?"

"I want to eat fondue till I'm sick. Oh, and I want to go to the catacombs."

Well, that was romantic. "The catacombs?"

"Oh yeah. And of course I would want to see all the Parisy sights too. The Eiffel tower, the Louvre, you know."

He didn't know. Not really. He'd had layovers in Paris, but he'd never explored much. "Here we are—whoa …" His truck slid, and he tapped the brakes a few times, trying to catch on something so he didn't end up parked in her parents' kitchen. Finally, the truck stopped. "Don't watch me try to turn this thing around. It's not going to be pretty." He was nervous again. That was okay. He couldn't think of a date to ask her on. He wasn't sure western South Dakota had anything resembling the catacombs. Wonderland Cave was a maybe, but it was closed in March, and he didn't think there were many skeletons down there. At least, he hoped not.

She looked him in the eyes, and he was again struck by her beauty. "Thank you so much for rescuing me." She gathered up her things and reached for the door handle. Then she looked at him again. "Really. I'm grateful. Things could have gone very wrong."

He nodded, having trouble finding his tongue. She was already out of the truck and about to shut the door when he found it. "When the sand trucks get out, I'll call for a tow truck."

She stopped, looking surprised.

Had he overstepped? "I'm sure Callum knows someone," he said lamely.

She smiled. "Thank you. I appreciate that." She shut the door and headed toward the house.

He waited until she was safely inside to commence the seventeen-point-turn it was going to take to get him out of this small, icy space.

He sighed. So what if he didn't get to take her on a real date? Maybe that was just as well. This had been fun anyway. A mini date. That's really all he should be having anyway. He couldn't go falling in love with a local girl.

Chapter 7

♥

S unny peeked out through the curtains. Patrick had told her not to watch, but she couldn't help it. She wanted to make sure he got out of her driveway. The rain was coming down in sheets. Some of it was freezing on contact, and some of it wasn't, creating the world's most dangerous Slip 'N Slide. She'd slipped twice on the way into the house, scared to death she was going to fall on her keister in front of Patrick Bannon.

But she hadn't. She'd gotten inside, given her dad a six-word explanation of where her car was, and then returned to watch Patrick maneuver out of her yard.

He backed up six feet, turned the wheel, and pulled ahead four. Then he backed up six feet, turned the wheel again, and pulled ahead. She didn't know whether to laugh or cry. She'd gotten him into this mess. She couldn't imagine he was enjoying it. Maybe she should have invited him inside. She cringed at the thought. Yeah right, like he'd want to come in here and hang out when he had a mansion to get back to.

Finally, he got the truck pointed in the right direction—she didn't know how he'd managed it with so little traction—and started up the driveway. She was both relieved and sorry to see him go.

She started to step back from the window. Wait. Why was he stopping halfway up the driveway? And why was he backing up? Oh, he wasn't backing up. He was sliding. Oh no. She held her breath.

The sideways, backward slide happened in slow motion, but that didn't make it any easier to stop. She braced herself as her dad stepped up behind her.

"Uh-oh," he said. "He's not going to make it."

Patrick's rear left tire slipped off the driveway, and the truck stopped.

"Go invite him in. He can wait here till the rain stops."

Oh, terrific. She let the curtain fall and turned to look at her dad. "When's that supposed to be?"

His nod said that he understood the nuance of her question. "Probably tomorrow morning, but don't worry. We'll make the best of it." He stood up straight. "I'll be on my best behavior."

She chuckled dryly. "You're not the one I'm worried about."

"Oh, your mother will be all right. She'll be thrilled to have a Bannon in the house."

Sunny wasn't so sure. She put her coat back on and stepped back out into the wind. She didn't really want to walk all the way to the truck. She wasn't sure she could do it without falling. She was grateful that Patrick was already climbing out of the truck. She waved him over. He turned his collar up and, his back hunched and his face turned away from the wind, headed her way.

She stood there shivering until he got there. "Come on in," she called over the weather.

She stepped into the kitchen and held the door open for him.

He quickly stepped inside and straightened, which made it seem like he grew a foot. He took his hat off, and water poured off the brim and onto the floor. He shivered. "Wow, that was a smidge chilly." He looked at her. "I think it's gotten worse out there since I left my house."

"Sorry," she said, meaning it with every cell of her body. "But you're welcome to stay here until ..." She didn't know how to finish the sentence. Until what? The rain stopped? He could get some salt delivered?

He smiled broadly, and boy, was that smile dazzling. "Till what? Spring?" He noticed her father standing on the other side of the room.

"Come on in," he said jovially. "Make yourself at home."

"Thank you, sir." He hesitated. Then he looked down at her. It seemed he didn't quite know what to do with himself. She knew the feeling.

"Can I take your coat?"

He nodded and shrugged out of it. She took it off his back, surprised at its weight. It was soaked. She couldn't remember a rain like this. She started to hang it up but then thought better of it. "Let me put this near the register so it will dry faster."

"Thank you." He followed her to the register and put his hat beside the coat. Then he stood there looking at her.

Good gravy, this was awkward.

"Can I get you something to eat or drink?" She couldn't believe Patrick Bannon was standing in her parents' kitchen.

He opened his mouth to answer her but was interrupted.

"Well, finally!" her mother cried from the other side of the room. "I've been waiting a long time to meet you!"

Chapter 8

♥

Patrick stared at the pretty woman in the long, flowing bathrobe. Sunny's mom. The artist. She certainly looked the part. But her declaration had confused him. She'd been waiting to meet him? Why?

"Mom, this is Patrick B—"

"I know who he is!" she cried, striding gracefully into the room. She reached out and grabbed one of his hands in both of hers. "This is your secret boyfriend."

A dozen questions ran through his mind at once, careening off each other like bumper cars. Sunny had a secret boyfriend? Who was he? Why was he a secret? How long had she been dating him? Was it serious—

"No, Mom. This is Patrick *Bannon*. You know, from the Bannon Ranch? Brooke married his brother?"

Her mother's eyes registered some understanding, but she still appeared overjoyed to see him. And she didn't let go of his hand. "Yes, yes, of c—" Her smile dropped jarringly, and a grimace took over her face as she let go of his hand and stepped back. "Oh, my. I understand now."

What exactly did she think she understood? Whatever it was, she didn't like it.

"I get it." She glared at Sunny, and Patrick immediately felt protective of her. What was going on? "You didn't want me to know you were dating a Bannon because you thought I'd be begging them for funding."

"No, Mom, I did *not* think that. Patrick is not my boyfriend."

"Stop lying to me!" she cried, sounding more hurt than angry. She put her hand on her chest, and her eyes filled with tears.

"Come on, honey," Sunny's father said gently. "Let's go sit down."

She slowly turned away and shuffled toward the doorway.

Patrick didn't fully understand what was happening, but this woman was genuinely upset. He looked at Sunny. "Do you have a secret boyfriend?" he mouthed.

She shook her head rapidly.

Phew. That was a relief. It also simplified things. He thought he knew how to make her mother feel better. He threw his arm around Sunny's shoulders. "I'm sorry, ma'am. But Sunny's not lying."

Everyone stopped moving. Sunny stopped breathing. Her mother slowly turned back around and then stared at him expectantly. He wasn't quite sure where he was going with this, but it was working so far. She'd already stopped crying.

"This is my fault," he continued, trying to think of how to say what he wanted to say without lying. "You are right in inferring that I'm quite fond of your daughter, but ..." His mind scrambled for words. "But I didn't want her using the word boyfriend. Not yet. I like to take things slow."

Sunny's mother's eyes grew wide, and her grin returned. Her husband, who had been trying to guide her out of the room, dropped his hands and stepped back, looking baffled.

"Can we start over?" He let go of Sunny and walked to her mother. He held out his hand. "Hi, I'm Patrick Bannon." He looked back and winked at a bewildered Sunny. "Your lovely daughter's *friend*."

She shook his outstretched hand. "I knew it!" She gave Sunny a triumphant look. Patrick didn't dare look at Sunny again. He hoped he wasn't overstepping, but this seemed a simple solution. "Come in, come in, sit!" She started toward the living room.

Unsure of what to do, he looked back to Sunny. Was she following? No. She stood stock still, her face pale.

Her mother stopped walking and turned to him. "Are you coming?" It was more of a demand than a question.

He almost laughed. She could be a bit bossy! He didn't know what to do. He didn't want to follow her and leave Sunny standing in the kitchen. He waited for her to move.

Her mother must have sensed the hold up. "Sunny, dear, why don't you get supper started while I talk to Patrick?"

Um, that wasn't going to happen. "You know what? It seems I'm going to be here awhile thanks to the weather, so how about if I help Sunny with supper and then we can all talk?"

Sunny's mother's face registered disappointment, but Sunny looked relieved.

"All right. But hurry up."

"Yes, ma'am."

She narrowed her eyes at him. "I appreciate your manners, but we're practically family. Call me Gloria."

He smiled. "Lovely to meet you, Gloria."

She stared at him for a disconcerting moment and then spun away. "Straighten up the living room, would you, Harold? I'm going to go get dressed. No one told me we were having guests!" And she was back to angry.

Sunny's father gave him an apologetic look and then left the room, presumably to go tidy up the living room.

Suddenly nervous, Patrick turned to Sunny. "Sorry," he said at the same time as she said, "Thank you."

She giggled.

"You're welcome. It just seemed simpler to go along with it than to try to argue. And she was so sad!"

"She's going to be *really* sad when you go back to Africa."

"Nah, it's the perfect cover. Then when you do meet Mr. Wonderful, you can dump me with an email, and we don't have to act anything out." He chuckled uncomfortably. He'd been joking, but talking about her dumping him didn't feel humorous.

She chewed her lip and looked at him thoughtfully. It seemed she was going to say something, but she didn't.

His phone rang. Shoot. He'd forgotten to tell anyone that his truck was stuck. "Excuse me," he said to Sunny before answering. It was Callum. "Yeah, I'm okay. I slid off Sunny's driveway, so I'm just going to hole up here for a while."

Callum hesitated. "Do you want us to try to get some salt and sand over there?"

"No, that's okay. The roads are awful. We can just wait till the weather lets up. Then you can come rescue me."

"Okay. Let me know if anything changes." There was a weird tone to Callum's voice, but Patrick didn't spend much time trying to analyze it.

"Thanks. I will." He hung up and looked at Sunny. "Okay, let's get supper started."

"You're really going to help?"

"Of course. What did you think, I was just going to mooch off you?" He smiled again. It had been a while since he'd smiled this much.

She went to the refrigerator. "Well, I'm a little embarrassed by what's on the menu. I was planning on Tuna Helper."

"What's wrong with Tuna Helper?"

"I don't like it, that's what. I was looking forward to some mac 'n cheese, but Mom wants Tuna Helper."

"Oh. And do you keep your tuna in the refrigerator?" He was no tuna expert, but it seemed she was looking in the wrong place.

She pulled out a bag of carrots, shut the fridge door, confidently clomped across the kitchen, still in her heavy winter boots, and pushed the carrots into his chest. "We still need a vegetable. So, *peel*."

He laughed and took the carrots.

As she walked to the pantry, she said, "You're a peacemaker, huh?"

"I've been accused of that before, yes. Where's your vegetable peeler?"

"Top drawer. I've been accused of it too. It's a good quality, but it can be tiring."

Didn't he know it. He opened the top drawer, which was chockablock with treasures. He rummaged around till he found a peeler and then saw two. They were identical, so he didn't spend much time choosing between them. He shut the door and set the bag on the counter. "I'm the middle child. Well, I guess Shane and I were tied for the honor. But I've always been the *nice one*." He made air quotes around the phrase. "Anyway, I learned early on how to diffuse conflict. Callum and Liam were always trying to kill each other, and Finn and Deedee, well, that could be ... dramatic."

She laughed. "And now Callum and Liam work side by side every second of every day."

"Yep. But now you know why Liam stays out of the office."

"I thought it was because he was addicted to fresh air."

"That too."

"What about you?" Suddenly she was right beside him, and it startled him because he hadn't seen her coming.

"What about me what?"

"Are you an indoor cat or an outdoor cat?"

Chapter 9

♥

Sunny's cheeks burned. Had she really just asked Patrick Bannon if he was an indoor *cat*? What was wrong with her? She'd meant it to be funny, but as soon as the words left her lips, she realized how ridiculous they sounded. He was a grown man. He didn't want to be called a cat.

"I'm definitely an outdoor cat," he said proudly, "but unlike Liam, I am able to function indoors just fine."

She giggled nervously. Good, he wasn't offended. Wondering why she was so nervous, she busied herself getting the Tuna Helper started as he peeled carrots at the counter. Hoping two boxes would be enough, she ripped into them and dumped the noodles, powder, and milk into a giant skillet. Then she went back to the pantry to get tuna. She cussed softly. She thought it had been softly enough that Patrick wouldn't have heard her, but that wasn't the case.

Suddenly he was right behind her. "What's wrong?"

"I can't believe this, but I think we are out of tuna." She groaned. "Who runs out of tuna? It's a cheap staple. It's what you have on hand for when you run out of everything else."

"May I?" Patrick gestured toward the pantry shelves.

Sunny nodded and stepped back out of the way.

Patrick stepped closer and started rummaging around the shelves. He pulled out a Ziploc bag of dried mushrooms and held it up to his face. "What are these?" He sounded horrified.

She giggled. "Morels."

"Morals? As in the moral of the story?"

Her giggle gained steam. "No. Morel mushrooms."

He raised an eyebrow. It was a cute expression. He looked so innocent, almost naive. "Are these *special* mushrooms?"

Her giggle turned into a gut laugh. "What? No!" She tried to take her mushrooms away from him, but he playfully dodged her grasp. "They're just mushrooms. We eat them."

He wouldn't let her grab them. Instead he pulled them to his chest, and her hand accidentally bumped into him. She pulled her hand back quickly, as if she'd been stung. *Awkward.*

"Can't we use them as a substitute for tuna?" he asked, looking at them more closely. "Where did you get them?"

"I picked them."

"Really?" He looked impressed, and she didn't know why. It wasn't hard to pick mushrooms. "And then you dry them?"

"Yes. In a dehydrator. And they are nearly a year old now, so we probably ought to use them up."

"Perfect." He held the mushrooms in one hand while he continued to rummage with the other.

"Now what are you looking for?

He shrugged. "I'll know it when I see it." He pushed a few more cans aside. "Probably don't want corned beef hash," he muttered.

She would have laughed at that if she weren't so terrified of what he was going to find lurking in the back of her parents' pantry. She'd never dug as deep as he was now digging. His arms were impressively long.

"That's weird." He pulled out a pill bottle.

She snatched it out of his hands, verified it was the one she'd picked up a week ago, and then shoved it into her pocket. She looked at him sheepishly. She didn't know what to say.

"Can't blame her," he said softly. "I don't like taking medicine either."

"She's not crazy, I promise."

He looked genuinely concerned. She became aware of how close she was standing to him. "Hey," he said. "I never suggested that she was."

Sunny nodded as her eyes grew hot. "She's just ... well, she marches to the beat of her own drum."

He turned his attention back to the shelves. "Nothing wrong with that. I've been accused of that myself."

This statement made her curious, but she didn't want to prolong his pantry search, so she pressed her lips together.

"Hey!" His excitement worried her.

She had a right to be worried.

He pulled a can of smoked oysters out of the dark depths and held it up beside his face like a trophy. The joy on his face appeared to be a hundred percent authentic.

"You can't be serious."

He looked at the can, confused. "What? It's perfect. We'll cut them up into tiny pieces. No one will ever know."

"*I'll* know."

He laughed, but as she continued to stare at him, his laughter died off. "Are you really going to make me keep looking?"

She was at a crossroads. Both paths were embarrassing. She glanced into the pantry, wondering what other forgotten tidbits lurked in there. Then she turned her eyes to the can. "What's the date on those?"

He checked ... and then grimaced. "They're only a little old."

She laughed. "What's a little?"

He swung the can behind his back and shut the pantry door with the hand that still clutched her mushrooms. "Too little to matter. Trust me. It's going to be delicious." He turned and headed toward the frying pan. Then he looked around. "I'll need a cutting board."

"What, are you taking over? You're supposed to be peeling carrots."

He smiled, and her knees went weak. Had she ever seen such a joyful smile in her life? Those lips ... those teeth ... that man knew how to spread happiness. "Do *you* want to cut the oysters up into teeny tiny bits?"

She laughed and pointed her eyes at the cutting board. "Right there. Help yourself." She went to the carrots and picked up the peeler. Fine, he could be in charge of supper. If she had to fast for the evening, she would. Or she would sneak into the kitchen in the middle of the night and have an ice cream nightcap. She started peeling. "You seem awfully comfortable with improvising."

"Well, when times are hard ..."

"What do you know about hard times? You're a Bannon."

When he didn't answer, she realized he was staring at her and looked up.

"I live in West Africa."

"Oh yeah." She started peeling again. "Sorry, I forgot."

He chuckled.

She peeled in silence for a minute, trying not to look at him, which was hard because he was bent over the cutting board like he was trying to win an especially challenging game of Operation.

The silence got to her. She was more comfortable with awkward chatter than with utter silence. "So, you have to improvise a lot in Africa?"

"Sure do. What I wouldn't give for a crate of smoked oysters."

When she didn't laugh, he turned toward her. "Kidding. Mostly."

She smiled. "I kind of pictured you living like a Bannon over there. You know, still rich." She cringed. Had she just said something rude? Sometimes she did that by accident. It was her overly honest gene. She knew whom she'd inherited that from.

"I have everything I need, for sure. Ma and Callum make sure of that." He didn't sound offended. He'd finished his operation and dumped the oysters into the pan.

No going back now.

He stirred the concoction and picked up the mushrooms. "Should we rehydrate these or something?"

"Nah, they'll be chewy, but they're good."

He shrugged and dumped some out on the cutting board. Then he bent to the task again. Were his eyes bad? Why did he have to get so close to what he was cutting?

"Anyway, we have trouble getting supplies in sometimes, and we don't ever live in splendor. That would be a disaster. It would make it harder to build relationships, and we would get robbed. Or worse."

"Is it dangerous there?"

"Not where I am. Not usually. I mean, there are some dangers, like snakes and mosquitoes—"

She snorted, and he looked up quickly.

"Mosquitoes?" she repeated. She'd thought he'd been joking.

"Yes, they carry malaria."

"Oh! That's right. I knew that. Sorry." She would have smacked herself on the forehead, but her hands were too busy. "Goodness, you've been there for years. Thank goodness you haven't gotten malaria yet." She looked up quickly. "Have you?"

"Nah," he said without looking at her. "I take medicine to protect me. It gives me trippy dreams and hallucinations."

Maybe that's why he was bent so closely to the cutting board. Maybe he thought the mushrooms were moving around, trying to get away. She bit back a smile.

"That's one of the medicines I don't like taking."

"Fair enough."

He'd just about finished chopping the mushrooms, so she transferred some carrots to his cutting board. "These need to be chopped too, while you're at it."

"Okay, but they're not going into the pan, right?"

"At this point, they might as well." She feared he would take her seriously. "But no."

Chapter 10

♥

Patrick couldn't remember the last time he'd had so much fun. And this was despite the fact that this was the dullest knife he'd ever worked with in his entire life. He might as well be trying to push a spoon through the food. The oysters were the worst as they squished under the pressure. The carrots were easier—but only a little. He took his time, trying not to slip and gash his fingers wide open. That's just what he needed in an ice storm.

Sunny put a new pot on the stove and then turned the burner on.

He stared at her profile. Her hair hung across her face, and it was all he could do not to reach out and brush it away.

She caught him looking. "For the carrots," she said, as if he were an idiot.

"Okay," he said—like an idiot.

She turned and leaned back against the counter, her arms folded across her chest. "So, you said you march to the beat of your own drum. Are you referring to the fact that you chose to leave your family's legacy and move to the jungle?"

He laughed. "Yeah. That, and more. I was always a little different than the others."

"Really? How so?"

She sounded genuinely interested, and this made him feel good about himself. It had been a while since someone other than his mother had wanted to know more about him. But that didn't mean he knew how to answer her. "I don't know. A little ... softer, maybe? I mean, I don't want to emasculate myself, but you know, I was the only one who wanted to take piano lessons."

"You play the piano?"

He laughed. "No. Sure don't. But there was a time when I wanted to."

"I'm surprised Shane didn't want to take piano lessons."

"He was already playing guitar by then. He said piano was a girl's instrument."

"Aw, that's not cool."

"Yeah." He chuckled. "And that's why I stopped taking lessons."

"Never too late to start again."

He nodded. It had been a long time since he'd thought about the piano. "This is true, but I don't have a piano in Africa, so it'll have to wait a little longer." He dumped the rest of the carrots into the second pot.

"What else?"

"Well, I ... I don't know." He looked at her. "You ask hard questions."

She smiled brightly, and it lightened the room. "You're welcome."

He laughed. "I love our ranch. It's our home. But I guess I was always just a little less excited about actual ranching than the others. I mean, Finn isn't excited either, but he's not excited about anything."

"Do you like horses?"

He shrugged. "Horses are a part of life. They're a part of who I am. But no, sorry, I don't have the urge to go hang out with them like Liam does or to trade them and breed them like Callum or ride them for fun like Deedee."

"I like horses."

He smiled at her. "Okay."

She looked embarrassed and gathered up the dishes from the counter. She dumped them into the sink and then came back to stir the tunaless Tuna Helper. "I can't even imagine what this is going to taste like."

"It's going to be delicious."

She gave him a dubious look. "What do you eat in West Africa?"

He shrugged. "Rice, beans, corn, plantains ... lots of dry cereal."

She looked surprised.

"It keeps well."

"Do you have milk?"

"We have goats."

She stared at him as if he were the most interesting thing she'd seen in a while. "I think I would like to try West African cuisine." Her voice went up a few notes when she said this, as if she were trying to sound like high society.

"You'd like it ... if you like a burning tongue."

"Oh yeah? Is it spicy?"

He nodded. "How do you think my hair caught fire?"

She laughed hard then, and this made him happy. He usually wasn't the funny guy. That was Finn's territory. "How long are we supposed to let this medley simmer?"

She sniggered. "Medley. That makes it sound like it will be harmonic."

"It will be. Music for the taste buds. You'll see."

She didn't look convinced. She went to the rubbage can and picked up the box. "Fifteen minutes," she read. She looked up. "Has it been fifteen minutes?"

"I have no idea. Hand me a spoon."

She did, and he lifted the lid to scoop out some noodles. He blew on them but still burned his tongue when he sampled them. Mmm, not bad. Salty. He wiped his mouth. "They're perfect."

She sniggered again. "I highly doubt that. But I'll go get my parents."

"Where are the plates? I'll set the table."

Chapter 11

♥

Sunny tried to walk like a normal person as she headed down the hallway toward the living room. She did not feel like a normal person. She didn't feel like herself—like her calm, cool, confident self.

Instead, she felt overly aware, as if every cell of her body was on high alert, as if she were made up of several strings and each of them had been plucked, everything vibrating at a thousand different frequencies. She felt wobbly and was tempted to look down to make sure her feet were touching the floor. She didn't, though. Obviously her feet were touching the floor because she was making forward progress. Thank goodness. She didn't need Patrick to come running to the rescue because she'd collapsed into a heap on the floor.

What was going on? She'd been around handsome men before. And she'd never responded like this. What was her problem? Maybe it was that Patrick was more than handsome. He was kind and funny too. A winning combination if there ever was one.

But there was something else going on. Something more.

She knew it wasn't his money. Lots of women in the area went all gaga over the Bannons, but she had never been one of them. Sure, she'd admired Liam's high cheekbones on occasion, but that had nothing to do with his wallet.

And this wasn't Liam. This was Patrick. A whole different ball of wax. He was so different from Liam. Different from everyone. He was warm, mysterious, sweet …

"Oh dear!" her mother cried from her spot by the window. "Why on earth were you keeping him a secret?" She looked at her husband and laughed. "I was afraid she was dating someone dreadful—a drug dealer or a lawyer—and that's why she wouldn't tell us anything. But he's not dreadful at all! I mean, I've never been a big fan of ranchers, necessarily, but if you're going to go for a rancher, it might as well be a Bannon. I mean—"

"Mom, please."

She stopped. This was surprising. Usually she didn't stop until she'd made her point, and then made a point adjacent to it, and then said something unrelated that, in her mind, supported said point.

"Supper is ready."

"Well, I'm not very hungry, but if your beau is staying, then I suppose I can be cordial." She stood, and Sunny saw that she had changed. She wore lovely, loose slacks with a matching top draped over it. She'd put on a chunky necklace and about two dozen bracelets.

"You look nice, Mom."

Her smile slid away, and she rolled her shoulders back. "I know how to look nice. I'm not some rube."

"No, Mom. I know that."

"She didn't insult you." Her father stood up. "She gave you a compliment. Stop imagining offense." He reached out and took her hand. "Come on, darling. Let's go eat supper." He looked at Sunny. "Tuna casserole?"

Sunny wasn't sure how to answer that simple question. "Sort of."

Her father stopped, appropriately confused.

"Patrick made it."

Her mother gasped. "He cooks too?"

Sunny couldn't help but smile. Not exactly. He innovated. She had no idea if he could cook. Someday she'd like to challenge him with a grocery bag full of traditional staples and see what he came up with. But that wouldn't happen, would it? Because Patrick lived in Africa. The loss of this imaginary cooking date brought her more sadness than it should have. She needed to back her heart away from this man, or the pain was going to be significant.

She followed her parents into their kitchen, where Patrick had set the table.

"I hope you're not offended …" Her mother sat down.

Sunny braced for the end of that sentence. Her mother didn't like to tolerate offenses, but she could sure dish them out.

"But we don't say grace in this house."

Sunny exhaled. That could have been much worse.

Patrick smiled, and it looked sincere. "That doesn't offend me in the least."

This concession should have ended the conversation, but of course, it didn't. Not with her mother.

"It's not that I don't believe in the possibility of a higher power. I do. I just don't see the point in giving her credit for canned tuna."

Patrick gave Sunny a charming look, his eyes flashing as if they had a particularly delectable secret between them.

Sunny pulled her chair out and sat down, trying not to be so aware of the man standing in her kitchen.

Patrick waited for everyone else to sit first and then took the only empty chair.

And she couldn't help watching him do so.

Chapter 12

♥

No one said a word about the missing tuna.

Patrick tried to enjoy his salty medley *without* staring at his hostess, but he could barely pull his eyes away from her. If he only looked at her face, she was only pretty—it was the rest of her that made her so ravishing. But it was more than her graceful body. It was her spirit shining out of her. She was obviously a happy woman, comfortable with herself, confident without being arrogant—she was amazing.

"So, Patrick, what do you do at the ranch?" Gloria asked.

Patrick felt Sunny stiffen at the question. He swallowed and let his fork rest on his plate. "Not much. I actually don't work there."

She nodded, unsurprised. "I wouldn't think you would need to work." She went back to her food.

Patrick picked his fork back up. That conversation had been far shorter than he'd expected it to be. He'd expected more questions.

A minute later, his expectation was met.

"So what do you do with your time then?"

Oh boy. He'd hoped not to discuss his work with this woman, but he wasn't going to be able to dodge it.

"Mom, Patrick doesn't have any time. He's a missionary."

Gloria didn't try to hide her shock. "A missionary? Where?"

"West Africa," Sunny said, sounding like she was ready for a fight.

Gloria's fork clanked on the plate, and she leaned back in the chair. "A missionary," she said, speaking to no one. She stared at him for a long time, long enough that he began to regret that his food was going to get cold. He was just about to resume eating even though she was staring at him when she turned her eyes on Sunny. "One of the Bannons is a *missionary?*"

Sunny surprised him with a laugh. "Yes, Mom."

Gloria turned back to him again. Darn. He'd missed his opportunity to take a bite. "Do you have a castle over there?"

"What? Mom, no!"

"Well, does he live in a hut? You're telling me that a filthy rich rancher's kid decides to take a vow of poverty and go live in a *hut*?"

"He didn't take a vow of poverty."

Patrick thought he should help Sunny, somehow, but he wasn't sure what he could or should say. This was one weird, unpredictable conversation.

"So, how do you live?"

Sunny looked at him.

Uh-oh. He was going to have to participate in this weird, unpredictable conversation. "I live in a small home with the other people who serve there."

Gloria looked at her daughter. "That's the definition of a vow of poverty!"

All right. Enough. He leaned forward and rested his arms on the table. "I live like any other missionary. My family supports our whole team. They send supplies. They make what we do possible. So no, there is no vow of poverty. I have not denounced my family or their wealth or anything else."

Her expression relaxed. She didn't seem quite so aghast. She nodded slowly. "And what you do, what they make possible … what is it, exactly?" She spoke slowly, as if she was trying to sneak up on him with her words.

"We help people. We have a small health clinic that focuses on natural healing and nutrition counseling, but we also have first aid capabilities. And we have helped people get clean water. We offer English classes. And of course, we tell people about the love of God."

She leaned back in her chair, looking defeated. "And here I was refusing to say grace."

No one replied to that.

"To a missionary."

He smiled. "It's really all right." And it was.

Gloria looked at her daughter. "You're dating a missionary?"

Oh boy. Maybe his ruse hadn't been a good idea.

Sunny smiled sweetly. "As he said, we're not serious. He has to go back to Africa …" It seemed that there could be more to that sentence, but she didn't finish it.

Abruptly, as if she'd put down one mood and picked up another, Gloria leaned forward, picked up her fork, and said, "Well, then, I apologize for misjudging you. Seems you're quite the spectacular human being. So tell me all about the art in West Africa."

The change made his head spin.

She took a big bite of cold noodles and then looked at him expectantly as she chewed.

"Well, as you probably know, it's quite amazing. Colorful, celebratory. Lots of pottery and wood carving. And textiles, of course. A lot of times, their clothing is their art."

She nodded rapidly. "You should bring some of it here, sell it to raise money."

He smiled.

"He doesn't need to raise money, Mom," Sunny muttered.

"Well, bring it anyway. I'll buy it."

"Sure. I'll bring you something next time I come home."

Sunny looked at him quickly with an expression he couldn't quite interpret. Then she looked at her mother. "Tell us what you're working on right now."

Patrick was grateful that the spotlight had moved off him, and as her mother talked about her different projects, he was able to finish his goulash. It appeared Sunny was done too, though she hadn't eaten much, so he offered to take her plate when he stood to take care of his.

"Oh no, I'll get it," she said, her fingers brushing his when he tried to pick up her plate. She stood too, and Gloria stopped talking. It appeared no one was listening to her anymore. But Sunny asked, "Is that going to be a series?" and her mother kept talking as if she hadn't been interrupted at all.

They went to the sink together, and he started the water, but she put a hand on his arm. "Please," she whispered, "let me."

He shook his head. "I'll wash. You dry." It seemed today would be a day for doing dishes.

She accepted his offer and went back to her seat, presumably to wait for her parents to finish, which they soon did. Then she said, "Let me help Patrick with the dishes, and then I'll deliver dessert to the living room." It sounded as if she was talking to children.

Her father stood. "Don't be too long. I like dessert. Come on, darling." He helped his wife up, though it was obvious she didn't need it. Patrick found this sweet. Harold obviously cared very much for Gloria.

Sunny grabbed a towel off the oven door and started drying. When they'd left, she softly said, "I'm so, so sorry."

"No need to be sorry. We all have parents."

"I know, but my mom was interrogating you."

"Oh, I am so used to that. Believe me. People always want to interrogate the missionary."

She giggled. "I can imagine. Sorry if I did that to you too."

She hadn't, had she? "You didn't, but you can ask me anything you want whenever you want. I like talking to you." He caught himself. Whoa. Had that been too much? He did like this woman, but maybe he shouldn't be flirting with her. He didn't want to give her the wrong idea.

He still lived in Africa.

"I like talking to you too," she said softly.

He noticed his hands had slowed down. He was trying to make the dishes take longer, drag out the chore so he didn't have to move on to dessert, which was weird. Because he usually really liked dessert.

Chapter 13

♥

Sunny took the ice cream out of the freezer.

"Whoa, you buy in bulk, huh?" Patrick joked.

He had a point. They bought their ice cream by the bucket. "My dad really likes his frozen dairy."

"Can't tell by looking at him."

"No. He's got the metabolism of a hummingbird."

Patrick laughed, which made Sunny proud of herself. "I am picturing your father flitting around from one pail of ice cream to the next."

She grinned as she struggled to scoop out the hard treat.

"Want me to do it?"

She tried to give him a dirty look, but she couldn't stop smiling. "Are you suggesting that I'm too weak to scoop ice cream?"

He took a step back and held up both hands. "No way. I would never call you weak."

She narrowed her eyes at him playfully. "Good, because chocolate ice cream is hard as a rock. If I'd known you were going to stare at me, I would have pulled out the vanilla."

He laughed. "Surely you're not suggesting that one flavor is easier to scoop than the other."

She widened her eyes at him. "I'd bet my life on it! Would you like me to pull out the vanilla and prove it?"

He laughed harder. "No, no, please. I take it back!"

Worried she might have been too aggressive with her defense, she tried to soften her voice. "Would you like some?"

"Sure. Two scoops, please. I know how effortless it is for you to scoop it, so you won't mind that second scoop."

She chuckled. He was messing with her, sure, but she would now throw her shoulder out of its socket if that's what it took to get this ice cream scooped faster. Because he was watching, she worked far harder at it than she normally would, and her arm was in fact growing tired. So tired that she was grateful when her mother came tearing into the kitchen with some new imagined crisis. "What is it, Mom?"

"We're going to have a black out." She grabbed the spaghetti pot, slammed it into the sink, and turned on the faucet. Sunny studied her. She often fixated on the worst-case scenario, but she also frequently had premonitions that turned out to be correct. Sunny wasn't sure which this was. "Why do you think the power's going to go out?"

"Have you looked out the window?" she cried.

"Yes, Mom. But the weather has been bad for hours now."

"Look at the power lines," she said without looking away from the filling pot.

Grateful for an excuse to take a break from the scooping, Sunny went to the front window. Ice was building up on the lines. "I see what you mean, Mom, but that's not too bad. Those lines are pretty tough."

Her mother snorted and then mumbled something Sunny couldn't make out. She didn't work too hard to decipher it. She let the curtain drop and turned to return to her ice cream, but now Patrick was scooping. The feminist in her was tempted to protest, but her arm muscles told the feminist to zip it.

"Get me another container!" her mother ordered.

Sunny sighed. She was getting tired. Normally she could ignore half of her mother's drama, but with Patrick here, it felt as if she was experiencing everything through his eyes as well. And she was starting to think her mother was being extra dramatic because Patrick was there. This probably wasn't intentional, but it was still annoying. "Mom, I think that pot will be enough. If the power goes out, they'll get it back up in no time."

"If the power goes out, they won't be able to get the trucks out because of all the ice.

"We could all go to the ranch," Patrick said. "We have a generator."

"How are we going to get to your ranch?" her mother snapped. "That's why you're stuck here!"

Sunny gasped, worried Patrick would be offended.

"Oh yeah." He licked a stray drop of chocolate ice cream off his hand. "Sorry, I forgot."

"Just get me another container!"

Sunny looked around. She didn't know what she wanted. The mop bucket?

"Do you have any empty ice cream containers?" Patrick asked her.

Oh yeah! "Good thinking." She went to the closet and found one, which she carried to the sink.

"Thank you," her mother said, sounding exasperated.

Patrick put the ice cream back into the freezer. Then he picked up two bowls. "Will you join us, Gloria?" He pointed his head in the direction of the living room.

She seemed torn: finish preparing for her imaginary crisis or go enjoy some ice cream with her daughter's imaginary boyfriend? Decisions, decisions.

She turned the faucet off. Ice cream had won. Again. "Fine, but I'll have to eat fast." She took a bowl out of his hand and headed for the living room.

Sunny gave Patrick an apologetic look, but he only smiled and swept an arm toward the hallway. "Ladies first."

This man was going to be the death of the feminist in her. "Thanks," she said and followed her mother.

Finally they were all settled comfortably in the living room, and, thank the heavens, no one was talking, as everyone's mouth was full of sugar. Sunny tried to relax and dug her spoon into the hard chocolaty goodness. She then put that spoonful into her mouth, and as the sweet treat hit her taste buds, half her anxiety melted away. She closed her eyes and leaned her head back to savor the flavor.

Her mother gasped, and Sunny's eyes popped open.

Their living room was as dark as a cave.

Chapter 14

♥

"I told you!" Gloria screeched. There was a crash, and, pointlessly, Patrick reached out with one arm to catch whatever was falling, but he didn't know what was falling, and he didn't know where it was falling to, so his arm just floated there uselessly. Grateful no one could see it, he pulled it back in.

"Darling, sit back down. Sunny will get a flash—"

Light burst from the cell phone in Sunny's hand.

Patrick looked around and still couldn't see what had made the crashing sound. But Gloria had moved from the couch to a chair. He looked at Harold. "Do you have a heater?"

He nodded. "In the basement. I'll get it." He stood.

Patrick stood too. "I'll help."

"No need. I can get it. But you could help by lending me one of those fancy phone flashlights."

Patrick took his phone out of his pocket and handed it over.

Harold looked at the black screen, flipped the phone over and looked at the back, and then flipped it front again. "How do I turn on the flashlight?"

Patrick took the phone back and did the honors.

"Thank you. Be right back."

"I'll get some candles." Sunny stood. Then she looked at Patrick. "Or maybe I shouldn't leave you two sitting here in the dark."

"We'll be fine," Patrick said. "You'll only be gone a minute."

Sunny didn't look so sure. "Okay. I'll hurry."

The room fell dark again, and sure enough, it was pretty weird sitting there in the black with Sunny's mother, who had chosen that moment to go silent. He wished she'd say something. Conversation would make the moment less weird. But she didn't say anything, and he couldn't think of anything to say either.

So they sat there awkwardly with only the howling wind to keep them company.

After eons, Sunny returned with candles. The lit one in her hand cast a light on her face that made her even more beautiful. Her blue eyes sparkled in the soft light.

Her father was right on her heels, and he plunked the world's oldest kerosene heater down onto the braided rug in the middle of the living room.

Oh boy. Patrick looked around the room. It was hard to see anything in detail, but it was an old house. He wasn't sure how well it was insulated. And was it already cooling off in there, or was that his imagination? He returned his attention to the heater Harold was fiddling with. Its apparent age wasn't necessarily a bad thing. He knew from experience that new appliances often broke more easily than the older ones, which were apparently built to last more than a few years.

But still. "Where'd you get that?" Patrick expected him to name one of the hardware stores in West Hope.

"Don't quite remember."

Oh dear. Had he inherited it? When were kerosene heaters invented? Was this a prototype?

"Sunny was just a baby, I know that."

This did not make him feel better. He wanted to ask how many square feet the heater covered but didn't want to insult the man. Besides, if he'd bought it thirty years ago, he probably wouldn't remember the appliance's specs. Patrick shifted in his chair. He'd thought this whole ordeal had happened by chance, but now he was glad God had plopped him down, here with the Bodeys. If this storm didn't let up, he might be of use to them.

Harold seemed to sense his doubts. "It's heated this whole house before. It will do it again." He got up, and Patrick realized he'd already gotten the heater going.

"Good to hear it," Patrick said.

Harold scanned the room till his eyes landed on his half-empty bowl of ice cream. He rubbed his belly. "But if we're going to sit around without power, we should eat the rest of that ice cream before it melts and runs all over the freezer." He looked at Gloria. "That would make a terrible mess."

Patrick didn't know if he was kidding.

Gloria rolled her eyes.

"You don't need any more ice cream, Dad. Eat what you've got." Sunny sat down and picked up her bowl.

There was nothing to do but fall in line and continue with his dessert. So they ate in the candlelight, as if nothing had changed, as if there wasn't a storm out there trying to ruin their night.

Chapter 15

♥

Sunny felt enormous pressure to say something, anything to fill the ridiculous silence. She couldn't believe she was sitting here, in the dark, with her parents and *Patrick Bannon.* She felt so bad for him. She couldn't believe she'd gotten him into such a predicament, and though he didn't look completely miserable, he had to be. Maybe he'd been through worse with all his missionary adventures, but she couldn't quite convince herself of that.

She tried not to stare at him, but her eyes kept darting his way, mostly to make sure he was still okay.

"So, Patrick, how do the Africans feel about you living there so you can push your religion on the—"

"Let's play a game!" Sunny blurted out.

Her mother looked at her in surprise. "A game?" She sounded delighted. This was good. That could have gone either way. "That's a lovely idea." She looked at Sunny's dad. "Do you want to play a game, Harold?"

"Might as well. It's either that or take turns watching television on our phones."

Sunny slid forward to get up.

"Why would we need to take turns?" her mother asked.

Dad chuckled. "If we all watch four different shows, none of us will be able to hear anything, and all our batteries will die at the same time. But if we took turns, we could make the batteries last a lot longer."

How long was he planning to be without power?

He looked around the room. "So, game? Or do we crowd around a phone?"

Sunny looked to Patrick for input. What did he want to do?

He caught her eye. "Oh, do I get a vote?"

"Of course you do!" her mother crooned. "Why wouldn't you? You get the biggest vote of all."

Patrick looked alarmed at that, as he should have. He looked at Sunny, and she tried to make her smile reassuring.

"We should probably save our phone batteries," Sunny said.

Her dad looked at each of them. "So, game?"

Sunny nodded.

"Okay, then." He stood up and crossed the room into the dark corner where the game cupboard lived. Sunny couldn't imagine how long it had been since that thing had been opened. She didn't play games with her parents, and they didn't have guests, not anymore.

Her dad came back for a candle and then returned to the corner and knelt to one knee with a grunt. "Monopoly?" he called out without turning around.

Sunny almost groaned. She didn't want to play Monopoly, but it might be their best option.

Her mother gave Patrick a playful look that was completely out of place. "I'm not much for capitalism, but it might be kind of fun to play Monopoly with a billionaire."

"What else is there, Dad?" Sunny could hear the desperation in her own voice.

"Clue?"

No one said anything.

"Candy Land?"

They still had *Candy Land* in their cupboard? Were they saving it for Sunny's children? The thing might disintegrate into dust by then.

"Life?"

"Oh, Life is fun," her mother said.

Sunny did not want to be sticking tiny plastic babies into a tiny plastic car with Patrick. That was just ... too weird, even for her. "What else is there?"

There was rustling as he slid boxes around. "We've got chess, but we'd be a knight short. Roxanne ate it, remember?"

Patrick's eyes grew wide. "Who's Roxanne?"

"She was our dog."

His eyes returned to their normal size. "Oh, that's a relief." He smiled. Still looked uncomfortable, though.

"Last time we played we used the Monopoly dog for the knight," her father said, sounding oddly proud of their ingenuity.

When was the last time they'd played chess, and how did he remember that detail? She turned to look at him. "Why didn't you use the Monopoly horse?" A horse for a horse, right? Made sense.

He gave her a sober look. "Roxanne ate that too."

"Is that what killed her?" Patrick said and then laughed.

Sunny looked at him in shock. Was he nuts? Her mother had loved that dog!

He squirmed in his seat. "It's a hard metal piece, right?"

No one answered him.

"Sorry for your loss," he said meekly.

"So, chess?" Her father was still waiting for a response.

"How are we going to play chess with four people, Dad?"

"I dunno. We could have a tournament."

She sighed. "No, Dad. A game of chess takes like an hour. We'd be bored out of our socks."

"Fine," he mumbled. "Excuse me for liking chess."

She caught Patrick's eye.

"A game of chess takes an hour?" he said.

She shrugged. "I don't know. I think it's supposed to."

He laughed softly. "I haven't played since I was a kid, but I was *really* bad at it. And it only took about five minutes for Callum to beat me."

Aha! So Patrick Bannon wasn't perfect. She had found his flaw. He was bad at chess. When he was a kid. "Callum was older than you. It probably wasn't quite fair."

He smiled at her, and it nearly made her dizzy. Those lips. "Thanks for trying to make excuses for me. But I'm sure he could still whip my butt now. I'm not very good at scheming."

"And Callum is?" Sunny said.

"Oh yes. Callum is a schemer."

"Invite him over!" her dad called out.

Patrick laughed genuinely. "Let's not."

"How about Pictionary!" her mother cried out, obviously having just thought of it.

Her dad groaned behind her. "Yea, that's in here."

"Then why didn't you say so?"

Sunny heard her dad stand up behind her and the cupboard door softly shut. "Because it's not really fair playing Pictionary with you."

"Oh, nonsense!" She popped up. "I'll go get my easel." She spun around and looked at her audience, the fabric of her outfit swinging after her, making the spin look like a choreographed dance move. "You two can be a team! We'll see who's smarter, young love or ..." She looked at her husband. "Old!" She spun again, the fabric creating a breeze, and she disappeared.

Her father sat down. "Has nothing to do with smarts. You guys are doomed."

Chapter 16

♥

Gloria clapped her hands together like a child and spun toward her easel. Her enthusiasm was adorable.

"Ready set, go," Sunny said and flipped the tiny plastic hourglass over. She was notably less enthusiastic than her mother.

Gloria whipped her marker across her giant piece of paper and then cried out, "Oh no!" She spun back toward them. "Stop the timer! This marker is dead. I've got to go get another one." She ran out of the room.

"Does she have a flashlight?" Patrick said. She hadn't taken a candle with her, which was a good thing because her speed would've blown the flame out.

"I don't think she does," Harold said. A crash in another room supported this theory.

Patrick waited for one of her family members to ask if she was okay, but they didn't. As he wondered whether he should check on her, she breezed back into the room carrying a new marker. "Start the timer!" And she was back at it. With a lightning quick hand she drew a pyramid with an arrow pointing to the top of it.

"Top Gun!" Harold declared.

Gloria cheered and shot both her arms up into the air.

"Seriously, Dad?"

Harold shrugged. "I knew it was a movie, and she pointed to the top so …"

Sunny looked at Patrick. "We really are going to get killed."

Patrick chuckled. "It's okay. Remember, Callum already taught me how to be a good loser."

She stood up. "Don't claim to be a good loser yet. You haven't seen how badly I draw."

"Oh, stop it," Gloria said. She gracefully sat down in the chair beside her husband's. "Art is in your genes."

Sunny shook her head. "Not this kind of art. Okay, someone start the timer." She said it like she was about to start a very hard test.

Gloria popped up, grabbed the timer, flipped it over, and gleefully yelled, "Go!"

Sunny stood staring at the blank page.

Patrick bit back a laugh. She was frozen, her marker in mid-air, pointed at the paper. He watched the sand drain through the tiny hourglass. "Do you want me to start shouting random movie titles?"

"I don't know what to draw. There's too much pressure." She was taking this way too seriously.

"*Rocky Three!*"

She giggled. He could barely hear her, but he saw her shoulders shake.

"*Pretty Woman!*"

She turned and looked at him. "Really? A big tough man like you, and that's the movie that comes to mind?"

He shrugged. "What? It's a good movie."

She turned back.

"Your time's half up." Gloria sounded nervous on her daughter's be-half.

Patrick gave her a few seconds to actually put the marker on the paper, but when she didn't, he offered, "*The Polar Express*!"

Sunny shook her head. "You sure do have a varied taste in movies."

He really wanted to come up with a movie that would make her accusation true. His brain scanned his memories, trying to think of something that would make her laugh. And then he had it. He blurted out, "*The Princess Bride*!" barely able to contain his excitement at the laughter he knew this would elicit. He was so proud of himself.

Sure enough, she doubled over with laughter.

"Well, I knew you two would be bad at this," Harold said, "but you're really outdoing yourselves."

"We might do better when it's my turn to draw. I'm not making any promises but ..."

Sunny started to unfold herself and gasped for air. "No ... No ... You don't understand." She held up the game card. "Look!"

At least, Patrick thought she said the word *look*. Her voice sounded like a squeaky dog toy that was leaking air after one too many teeth punctures.

"Look at what?" Harold said.

"It's *The Princess Bride*!" Sunny cried out, her words barely intelligible. She tipped back with laughter and then said it again. "He got it! *The Princess Bride*!" She straightened, and it appeared she was trying to get a hold of herself. This was a shame. Watching her laugh with such abandonment was a beautiful thing. She wiped her eyes with the back of her hand and then handed her father the marker. "Beat that." Most of the laughter was gone from her voice then, and the two words sounded downright threatening.

With good reason, Harold looked nervous as he took the marker from her outstretched hand.

Sunny neatly tucked the card back into the box and then gave Patrick a dazzling smile. "Nice work, partner." She collapsed on the couch as if she was exhausted, and Patrick could not pull his eyes away from her.

"This one is a food," Harold said. He still sounded nervous.

"Hang on." Patrick jumped up and took the timer, flipping it over on the way back to his seat. "Go."

"Okay, food." The marker squeaked across the page as Harold drew what looked like a human head with giant horns.

"Honey, what on earth is that supposed to be?"

"Wait!" Harold snapped. "Give me a second."

Gloria pressed her lips together, and Harold kept scribbling. After he finished drawing weird stripes on the horns, he wrote a plus sign and then drew what looked like a bowl. Then he looked at his wife expectantly. He pointed to the head, raised his eyebrows, pointed to the bowl, and then gestured impatiently for her to say something.

Patrick had no idea what that drawing was supposed to be.

"Mountain goat stew?" she guessed.

Harold's hands dropped to his sides. He tipped his head sideways and gave her a look of utter disappointment. "Who eats mountain goat stew?"

Patrick had eaten plenty of goat stew in his day, but he was staying out of this. He glanced at the hourglass. They were out of time, but he didn't want to stop the show. Harold stabbed his marker at the paper with force.

"Stop that!" she snapped. "You're going to ruin the marker! I don't have an endless supply!"

"Yes, you do. The clerks at Hobby Lobby know you by name." He pointed at the bowl-ish figure. "It's not stew!"

"Dad, you can't talk!" Sunny looked the timer. "You're out of time! Oh my stars, Dad, what *is* that?"

He pointed to the head-thing and said, as if they were all idiots, "Indian ..." Then he pointed to the bowl. "Pudding."

"Dad," Sunny said softly, "I think you just offended every Native American in the country."

Her father threw the marker at her. "Fine. Remember that I wanted to play chess!"

"Why did you throw the marker at me? It's Patrick's turn."

Patrick couldn't believe how much fun he was having. He got up. To think, just a few minutes before he hadn't been looking forward to playing games with this family in the dark. He pulled a card out of the box. What on earth? He looked at the card again and looked at the box. These cards looked homemade. "Is this even Pictionary?"

"Sort of," Sunny said softly. "My mother made it."

Patrick looked at Gloria in wonder. "You made your own game?" He picked up the box. It looked so real. "You're so talented."

"Yes, well, go ahead." Gloria had lost some of her enthusiasm, and Patrick worried that he had embarrassed her. Maybe she had made the game because they couldn't afford Pictionary at the time. How resourceful. He hurried to the easel before looking at what his card actually said. When he did look down, he was dismayed to see what it read.

"What's the category?" Sunny asked, a demanding edge to her voice.

"Food." He looked at the card. *Frog legs.* He looked at the paper. Could he even draw a frog? He shouldn't have been so critical of Harold's goat head. He took a deep breath and put his marker to the paper.

Chapter 17

♥

"All right." Sunny's mom came back into the room rubbing her arms. "It's too cold to sleep in the bedroom. Guess we're all going to have to bunk in here."

Sunny sneaked a peek at Patrick, wondering what he thought of this news. He appeared unfazed.

"Nonsense," Dad said and left the room. He was back minutes later with an armload of blankets.

"Oh, honey, we can get the sleeping bags out."

He dropped the blankets on the couch beside Sunny. "These aren't for people. I thought we could hang them in the doorways, try to trap this heat in here with us. It's not exactly balmy in here."

"You can't do that!" Mom cried. "The pipes will freeze."

Not responding to that worry, he pulled a package of thumb tacks out of his pocket, and Patrick jumped up to help him hang the blanket.

Sunny felt helpless. This was so out of control. Was Patrick Bannon really going to have to spend the night with them? In the same room? She got up and went to the front door. Halfway there, she had second thoughts. It was indeed cold in the kitchen. She didn't know if it was cold enough to freeze pipes, but it might be close. The kerosene heater was a long way from the kitchen.

She went to the front windows and looked outside. Of course, she couldn't see anything. She'd foolishly hoped the moon would help, but she'd forgotten that the moon didn't provide a lot of light when there were storm clouds in the sky. She opened the door and stepped outside, quickly shutting the door behind her, not that it mattered much. It was almost as cold in the kitchen as it was out here.

Her eyes adjusted, a little. The rain had turned to snow, and it was coming down hard. The wind seemed to have died down, but it was still blowing. She sighed. She didn't want Patrick to leave, but she wanted him to be rescued from this ridiculous situation she'd put him in. But it didn't look like that was going to happen anytime soon. She closed her eyes and listened for sounds of plow trucks or lineman trucks, but all she heard was the wind. Too cold now, she spun to go back inside and almost ran into Patrick.

"Whatcha doin'?" He closed the door behind him.

"Checking on the weather ... Dumb, I know, but I thought I might be able to learn something useful."

He was so close to her that she could feel the heat coming off him. "No, it makes sense. When we don't know what's going to happen and what's going on outside our little bubble, we can feel pretty desperate for information."

She tried to see his face in the darkness. "That was pretty profound."

"I can be profound."

Good grief, his face was kissing distance from hers—

Kissing distance? her brain screamed at her. "We should get back inside."

He caught her arm, and for one insane second, she thought he *was* going to kiss her. "I hope I didn't offend your mother when I said that thing about the game being homemade."

"Offend her? Why would that offend her?"

Breath rushed out of him. "Oh good. I wasn't even thinking about *why* she'd done it. I just thought it was so cool."

"Cool?" Sunny said and then wished she hadn't sounded so sardonic. She could barely make out his facial features and yet she knew he was confused. "Sorry," she mumbled and reached for the doorknob.

"Why wouldn't it be cool? She's so talented."

She stopped reaching. "I used to have a real Pictionary game, and there were things in the original game that my mother couldn't draw. This made her very upset. So she threw my game away, and she made a game, and she made a bunch of cards of only things she could draw. *That's* why my dad knew they would slaughter us. The deck was as stacked as it could get."

"Oh," he said slowly. "I thought it was that you guys couldn't afford the game at some point."

She snorted. "Who can't afford a ten-dollar board game?"

He didn't say anything, and she thought of all his friends in Africa.

"Sorry, that was insensitive. I suppose there are lots of people who can't afford a ten-dollar card game."

"No worries, and hey, we didn't exactly get *slaughtered*." He playfully bumped his hip into hers. "We held our own."

"I suppose."

"Also, sorry if I was crass about Roxie."

"Roxie?"

"The dog."

"Oh. Roxanne."

His face fell. "Okay, now I'm double sorry. I wasn't trying to be cruel. I do like dogs. I was trying to be funny."

"It's okay. You are funny. Usually."

"Hey, everybody swings and misses sometimes."

She doubted that he missed anything very often. He seemed to be very good at life. "Yeah."

He opened the door for her and put his hand on the small of her back. It was the warmest, most welcomed touch she'd ever had the pleasure of feeling, and she almost didn't move because of it, but then he applied some more pressure and she realized how weird it would be if she kept refusing to go inside.

He shut the door behind her, and the sole burning candle on the counter seemed so bright after the outdoor darkness.

"You know what," he said slowly.

"What?"

"It's pretty cold in here."

She giggled. "Good job, Sherlock."

He laughed. "No, really. I think your mom's right."

"That's not something I hear often. You mean about the pipes?"

He nodded. "Yeah, I think we should bring the heater in here." He looked at her quickly. "Totally up to you guys, of course. I don't live here, but that's what I would do."

"I think the plan was that we would all sleep around the heater like a campfire."

He nodded. "We can do that in here."

"In here?" she looked around. "Where?"

He scanned the room. "Yeah. It would be a bit tight."

A bit? They'd have to treat the kitchen table like a bunk bed.

Her dad came into the kitchen. "Oh, sorry. Didn't mean to interrupt." He started to back up.

"Dad, wait."

He stopped.

Patrick looked at her expectantly.

"What would you think about moving the heater in here? We could sleep in here too. It's not like we're going to get much sleep anyway." She certainly wasn't. She was trying to stave off falling in love. Not exactly a relaxing activity.

He seemed to be contemplating it. Then he let out a long breath and turned around. "Let me tell your mother."

As they followed him to the living room, the air grew warmer with each step.

Funny, when she'd left the living room, it had felt chilly in there. Now it felt wonderful. "Ugh. Maybe we don't want to lose all the heat we've gained in here."

Her father looked at her. "I'd rather save the pipes."

She didn't understand why the pipes were in such peril. "We've lost power before." She looked at the heater. "Didn't that thing do a better job last time?"

"I don't know," Dad said. "But it's been a while since we've lost power for this long, and that wind is something terrible."

"It's actually died down some now," Patrick said.

"Good." He looked at his wife. "We're moving to the kitchen."

"What?" she cried. "Why?"

He didn't answer her.

"But I'm tired! I was going to try to get some sleep!"

Her father looked at Patrick. "Could you help me carry the couch into the kitchen?"

The couch? Really?

"Sure." Patrick had his end of the couch lifted before her father had even bent over.

Normally, she would have insisted that her father let her do the heavy lifting, but she didn't want to insult him in front of Patrick. And it turned out there wasn't any need for her to interfere. The men moved the couch easily enough, and then it was plugging up almost all of the kitchen's floorspace.

Her father shoved the kitchen table up against the wall, and then Patrick followed him back into the living room.

Sunny looked at her mother.

"I'm sorry this is happening."

Sunny startled. She hadn't been expecting that. "That's okay, Mom."

"No, I'm sure you're quite embarrassed."

"Mom, for the zillionth time, I am not embarrassed of you."

"I didn't mean me. I meant your father."

This struck Sunny speechless, but as she tried to find her tongue, her mother laughed. Oh! She'd made a joke!

Patrick came back in with the heater and plopped it down where the centerpiece on the kitchen table had been just minutes before. This time, though, her father had trouble getting the heater going, and a small panic fluttered through her. What would they do if they didn't have the heater? Go sit in Patrick's stuck truck till it ran out of gas? Put on ice cleats and huff it to the Bannon Ranch? She didn't think they owned any ice cleats.

The heater kicked on, and she let herself exhale. She looked around the room. Now what? Were the four of them going to share the couch?

Chapter 18

♥

Patrick surveyed the scene before him, trying to figure out possible sleeping arrangements. He was getting tired, and despite Sunny's claim that none of them would be getting much sleep, he thought he'd be able to sleep just fine. He had spent plenty of nights in situations far less comfortable than this.

"I wish we had a cot to offer you," Harold said.

"Oh, nonsense." Gloria waved her arm in his direction. "Let the kids take the couch …" Her head snapped toward her husband. "Do you think you boys could drag Sunny's mattress in here?"

"And then where do I sleep?" Harold sounded almost paranoid.

Gloria rubbed her throat. "With me on the mattress, silly."

Harold rolled his eyes. "We're going to share a *twin*?"

Gloria tipped her head back and giggled. "Sure! We'll be fine." She waved her arm at Patrick again. "It's better than trying to share the couch. Let the young love birds cozy up on the couch. We'll make do with the mattress."

Oh boy.

"Son, would you give me a hand with a mattress?" Harold started down the hallway once again.

Patrick hesitated. Did Sunny really want him rooting around in her room?

"I'll help you, Dad!" She was off like a bolt of lightning, and once again, he was left to bond with Gloria Bodey by candlelight. Through the walls, there was arguing, banging, and one loud yelp. Then down the hallway they came, pushing a twin mattress. He hurried to give them a hand, but when they tried to lie the mattress on the floor, Patrick realized he needed to work on his spatial awareness.

It didn't fit. Not even close.

"Let's move some of these kitchen chairs into the hallway." Patrick picked one up and held it up over his head as he navigated toward the empty space.

No one else moved, so he returned for another chair. It became apparent that he was in this alone, and he moved the last two.

The mattress still didn't fit.

"The table's not going to fit in the hallway," Gloria cried, her voice full of accusation. "Not with all those chairs in there!"

Patrick sighed. The only way that table ever would have fit in that hallway is if they knocked out a wall. "I can stand it on its end?" No one argued, so he grabbed one end of the table and lifted. Then he pushed the top of the table up against the fridge. Its four legs stuck out like a dull *chevel de fries* trying to protect their leftover oyster helper.

Harold pushed the mattress, and Patrick jumped out of the way, nearly tripping over the couch. The mattress hit the floor with a soft thud. Moving the table had created quite a bit of room. They could probably even squeeze in a bigger mattress, but Patrick was not about to suggest that.

He realized Sunny had vanished. He looked around for her and then felt silly. If she were in this room, he would be able to see her without effort.

She breezed back into the room with her hands full. "We only have three sleeping bags, but you can have mine. I'll go find some blankets for me."

He wasn't sure how to handle this. He did not mind snuggling up next to a beautiful woman on the couch, and he knew he could keep the situation perfectly innocent, but he wasn't sure if *she* wanted him snuggling up to her. She hardly knew him.

Her parents distracted with rehanging the blanket in this new doorway, he knew this was his chance. Two quick steps had him right in front of her. He reached out for a sleeping bag but then didn't take it away from her. They just held it, both of them.

"I don't want to make you uncomfortable," he said quickly and quietly. "I can sleep in the hallway."

She looked horrified. "The hallway's going to be cold."

"I'll be fine." He tried to take the sleeping bag, but she held on.

"And hard."

He stopped tugging. "What?"

"The hallway. It's going to be a hard surface to sleep on."

"I'll be fine," he said again.

She stepped even closer. "Please, can we just share the couch?"

"Oh." He was surprised, but he tried to play it cool. "Sure. I just didn't want to—"

Her mother was coming toward them then, and Sunny interrupted him, "We can share the sleeping bag." She held another out to her mother.

"Aw." Gloria's eyes were sparkling. "You two are so sweet."

Patrick's cheeks got hot, and he was glad the lighting was dim. "Do you need help with anything else?" he asked, looking at Harold.

He shook his head. "Naw, let's try to get comfortable."

"Pillows!" Sunny cried and then disappeared again.

For lack of options, Patrick sat on one end of the couch. He tipped his head back. His eyelids weighed a ton each. What had he done today that had him so tuckered out? Was he still recovering from jet lag? He'd found that the older he got, the more the time zones tried to torture him.

He felt Sunny breeze back into the room and forced his eyes open. She'd doled out the pillows and was holding one out to him now. He took it.

"Go ahead, get comfy," she said softly. She sounded so sweet and innocent. "I can take the edge."

He wondered if they should have flipped the couch around, so the seat was against the wall. Then she wouldn't fall off. But he didn't want her pinned in either. So he lay down and pressed himself into the back of the couch as much as possible. Eying the space left for Sunny, he felt better about the situation. There was enough room.

She lay down in front of him, and her hair barely brushed against his face, christening his nose with jasmine.

Turns out there wasn't as much space as he'd thought.

She was very close to him.

He wasn't going to be sleeping much after all.

Chapter 19

♥

Why in the heavens does this man smell like black licorice? Sunny squeezed her eyes shut. She was never going to fall asleep like this. He was being a perfect gentleman, of course. She would expect nothing less.

But he was so *there*. She could feel his heat, which was welcome, the whole length of her body, and the scent of licorice enveloped her. Were his pockets full of jellybeans? What man smelled like sweet licorice?

Her wild-mushroom-canned-oyster-goulash supper was wearing off. She was starving. Maybe she should have let her father dish out the last of the ice cream after all. It was too late now, though. There was a table leaning against the refrigerator. And even if there wasn't, opening the freezer door would bonk her mother right in the head. She tried to slow her breathing, tried not to think about anything, tried to imagine she was staring at a blank gray wall, and tried to fall asleep—but there was a gorgeous man warm at her back and the smell of licorice in her nostrils.

"Are you okay?" he whispered.

"Yeah. Why?"

"Sorry. I thought you weren't breathing."

She didn't know what to say to that. Had she been breathing? Maybe not. She focused on inhaling and exhaling.

"I *really* don't want to make you uncomfortable," he whispered into her hair.

"You're *really* not," she whispered back. This was only sort of a lie. He *was* making her uncomfortable, but not in the way he thought.

They were quiet for some time then, but she knew he wasn't sleeping. She could feel that he wasn't relaxed. She felt bad about this, but she had no idea how to fix it. Apparently they were just going to lie there, stiff as two boards, till morning.

Suddenly, out of the still darkness, her father roared with a snore that could've woken the dead. She and Patrick both jumped, shaking the couch and knocking her back into his body. She grabbed the edge of the couch and rocked herself back to it, but that took an incredible amount of will power.

Had Patrick jumped from the roar or from her jerking the whole couch? She didn't know. But the couch was shaking as he silently laughed.

She sat up abruptly. This was stupid. She scooted down to the end of the couch by his feet.

He pulled his legs in slowly and sat up too—much closer to her than he needed to. "Sorry," he whispered, "I get dippy when I'm tired."

What? That didn't make sense. He wasn't being dippy. "You have nothing to apologize for."

"Yes, I do. A grown man has a right to snore in his own kitchen—" And then he was laughing again.

And it was contagious.

"Shhh, we'll wake them up." She realized her hand was on his leg, and as good as that felt, she pulled it back quickly.

He grabbed it and held it. She could feel him taking long, deep breaths. When he'd recovered, he still held her hand. What did that mean? It didn't necessarily mean anything, she told herself. He turned and looked at the far end of the couch. "I guess this sleeping arrangement isn't working, is it?" he whispered.

"It's not that," she said quickly. She didn't want him to move into the hallway. "I just have a hard time falling asleep, even on a good night."

"And tonight isn't a good night."

Her spirit sank. Actually, this *was* a good night. For her. It was the best night in a really long time. This was both absurd and embarrassing. Her life was pathetic. That was okay, she told herself. *You're not living your life for you. It's what you do for others that gives your life value.* Of course this wouldn't seem like a special night to Patrick. He was used to adventure. He was used to helping scores of people on the other side of the world. Helping her parents was nothing compared to digging wells in Africa.

"I'm so sorry that you're trapped here," she whispered.

"Oh, this isn't trapped, and honestly, I'm not as annoyed with any of this as you probably think I am. I've had fun tonight. It's an adventure."

Her spirit lifted at his use of the word *adventure*. "Still, though, you are, by definition, trapped."

"Not really." He sounded contemplative.

"We must have different definitions of the word trapped."

He sucked in some air. "You know, I used to have this young friend. His name was Abrafo. He was ten. He'd lost his mother, and he was so quiet, so shy. He always seemed sad. His culture practices polygamy, so he had other *mothers*"—he made air quotes with his free hand— "but they weren't very nice to him." Patrick sounded as sad as the kid he was describing. "From what I saw, his father wasn't really available to him, so he was lonely, and he took to me and to Jesus really quickly." She heard the smile in his voice. "We grew pretty tight. His village was about three miles away, and I made the trip as often as I could. Anyway, he could speak some English, but it was his second language. Well, we got a shipment of MP3 players with the Bible on them in his language. I didn't think he'd want one, he was so young, and I gave the few out that I had when I visited his village. He was so upset that he cried and cried, so of course, I promised I'd be back in a few days to give him one." He stopped talking and ran a hand over his face.

"You sound tired."

"Oh, I am so very tired." He chuckled quietly. "Anyway, before I could get back to him, we had horrible floods. All the roads, which were hardly roads to begin with, washed out, and our home flooded, and I was going stir crazy wanting to get back to him. I didn't want him to think I wasn't going to keep my promise." He paused. "It might not seem like a big deal, but then ... it was so huge to me then. I felt so guilty. I didn't want to be the reason his heart broke yet again. And if he started to doubt my love for him, then he might start to doubt Jesus' love. There was so much pressure ..." He paused, remembering.

It sounded like a lot of that pressure had come from Patrick himself.

"So I was stuck waiting, watching the rain, dragging my feet through the mud, waiting for the flooding to stop, and all I wanted to do was get back to him." He took a breath. "That ... *that* was trapped. This ..." He turned to her and smiled. "This isn't trapped." He squeezed her hand. "I'm not the least bit sorry that I'm here, and I'm in no hurry to leave."

Shoot. Her toes had reached the point of no return, and she'd gone screaming right past it. She was going to fall in love with this man. And while that felt amazing, it was not a good thing. He had to go back to the mission. He had to get back to people like this little boy. And though, if he asked her, she'd go with him in a heartbeat, there was no way she could leave her mother. And she couldn't leave her father to take care of her mother alone.

"The little boy ... he must have understood once you finally got back to him?"

Patrick didn't answer. Instead, he lightly dragged the tip of his thumb across the back of her hand, sending shivers up her arm. "He was gone," he whispered. His voice had changed.

"Gone? Gone where?"

"To heaven."

She looked up quickly, and his eyes shone with tears. She found herself desperate to comfort him, but she didn't know how to. "He died?" She wanted to slap herself. Way to state the obvious.

Patrick nodded. "Drowned. I don't know what happened, exactly. His village lost several people. I tried to ask his father, but he promptly dismissed me. Wanted nothing to do with me. Told me not to worry, that he had other sons."

She gasped. "That's awful."

He nodded. "Yes, yes, it was." He ran a hand over his face. "Sorry, didn't mean to get so serious." He forced a smile and squeezed her hand again. "Just trying to say that I'm not trapped here."

Before she knew what was happening, his lips were on hers, and they were warm and sweet and tender and perfect. She was only starting to relish the kiss when he pulled away, leaving her stunned and breathless.

He looked at the far end of the couch again and then looked at her. "Come on, let's try to get some sleep. Who knows what crazy the morning will bring."

She smiled at his phrasing and watched him lie down. He was just going to kiss her like that? Like it was no big deal? Like it was a perfectly natural thing to do? She forced herself to breathe, tried to make her heart stop pounding. She feared that if she lay back down next to him, he would be able to feel that pounding through her back—and that would be embarrassing. He certainly had a power over her, but she wasn't quite ready for him to know that.

He looked at her, and despite the dim lighting, she thought she saw concern in his eyes. "Are you okay?"

No, I'm not okay. You just kissed me, cowboy! She nodded quickly, "Yeah. Yeah." She wanted to slap herself. Had she really needed to say that twice? Begging her heart to calm down, she stretched out beside him, and this time, he wrapped his arm around her waist and pulled her into him. This made her so happy that she almost cried when he pulled his arm away, but he was only reaching down to pull the sleeping bag up over them, and then he slid his hand down across her stomach again and held her under the blanket.

"Is this okay?" he whispered, and her hair moved in his breath.

"Yes." It was so much better than okay. She hoped morning, and all its crazy, would take its sweet time getting there.

Chapter 20

♥

Patrick didn't want to wake anyone up, especially not Sunny, but he really had to go to the bathroom. He lay there as long as he could, enjoying the smell and feel of her hair on his cheek, but then nature won the standoff. As slowly as he could, he pulled his hand out from around her and then pushed himself up onto his left knee. He paused then, in case she stirred, but also because he wanted to admire her. When she didn't move, he swung his right leg over her.

As soon as it hit the floor, her eyes popped open and widened at the sight of him directly over her, straddling her, staring down at her. Good grief. "Sorry," he said quickly and sprang the rest of the way off the couch.

She sat up slowly and rubbed the sleep from her eyes. "That's okay. What time is it?"

"I was trying not to wake you up, and I don't know what time it is. Time to pee, I guess. I'll be right back." He went to the door and then stepped through it as fast as he could, not wanting to let any of their hard-earned heat escape.

The fresh air was bracing. He was now fully awake. Snow still fell, but the wind had died down. Good. Maybe they were on their way out of this thing. He walked across their yard, wanting to get far from their house before doing his business. He slipped twice before deciding he was far enough. The four inches of snow hadn't made the ice underneath it any less slippery.

His eyes had adjusted now, so he took in the scenery—the whole world blanketed in pure, undefiled white. It was quite a sight.

Grateful to be finished—it was still plenty cold out, even without the wind—he turned to go back inside, taking care with his footsteps.

When he got back inside, everyone was awake, and Gloria was panicking over coffee. She looked at him with wild eyes. "I'm serious. I will get *sick* if I don't have my coffee."

Patrick headed for the sink to wash his hands in the cool water.

"It won't be good for the rest of us either, darling." Harold still sat on the mattress on the floor. He looked at Patrick. "How was the outdoor plumbing?"

"Brisk." Patrick splashed some of the water on his face, wishing he had a toothbrush.

Harold grunted as he got up. "Still grateful to have it, I suppose." He headed for the door. "Could be worse. I could have a neighbor living ten feet away."

"Your phone rang." Sunny held Patrick's phone out to him. "I found it in the cushions."

"Oh no." He took it from her hand, allowing his fingertips to brush hers as he did so. It was going to be so hard to leave her. "Is that what woke everyone up?"

Sunny shrugged. "No big deal. It's morning."

He should have thought to turn his ringer off. He looked at his call history. One missed call from Callum. "Excuse me," he said to the ladies and dialed his brother back.

"How are you guys holding up?"

"Good." Patrick rubbed the back of his neck. "Trying to figure out how to make coffee with a kerosene heater."

"Do they have instant?"

Patrick looked up at Gloria. "Do you have instant?"

"Of course not! We're not barbarians."

He chuckled. "No, no instant."

"That's too bad. I don't know then. But hey, we've got everything plowed and sanded. Want us to come get you out? We've got coffee here."

"Are the roads clear?"

"Clear enough. I think we can get there."

"Well, then, yeah. What are you waiting for?" He smiled at Gloria. "Coffee's coming."

"I didn't say we'd *bring* you coffee."

"Well, please do."

"Okay, I'll tell Holden. I'm probably not coming, but I'll send a crew. And I'll tell Ma to make up a thermos."

"Send a tow strap. My truck is blocking part of the driveway."

"Will do, brother. Let me know if you think of anything else."

"Thanks, Callum." He hung up and tried to meet Sunny's eyes, but she wouldn't look at him. "The ranch has generators. You're all welcome to come back with me until the power comes back on."

"That's not necessary," Sunny said as her mother whooped with joy.

"Yes!" Gloria cried. "Thank you!" She came to him and flung her arms around him, squeezing him so tight he was surprised he didn't squeak.

He would have returned the embrace, but she had his arms pinned to his sides. "It's no problem, really."

Sunny still wasn't looking at him, or he would have silently pleaded for help.

Harold came back inside. "Gloria!" he yelped. "Why are you attacking Patrick?"

She let him go and held him at arms' length, smiling up at him. "Can I just tell you how grateful I am to you?"

He hadn't done anything except heat up some canned oysters.

She turned and looked at Sunny, who was studying the floor, and then back to him. "I don't know if Sunny has told you, but I struggle with anxiety." Her smiled faded. "It can get really bad. But let me just tell you how happy it makes me to know that she's found you—"

"Mom!" Sunny tried to stop her.

"I've never seen her so happy as she is when she's with you."

Sunny groaned.

"And it just makes me feel so safe knowing that she's happy and going to be taken care of." She let go of him, but she didn't back away. "Thank you for taking care of my daughter, Patrick. I can leave this earth knowing that she is safe and loved."

"Mom!" Sunny cried, standing up. "Stop!"

Gloria rolled her eyes.

"First, stop talking like you're about to drop dead. And second, how about you *don't* put a bunch of pressure on the man? We've explained that we're not serious. In fact, now's as good a time as any to tell you—"

Completely ignoring her daughter, Gloria spun toward her husband. "The Bannons have invited us to the ranch to wait out the blackout with them!"

Harold's eyes widened. "What?"

Gloria nodded wildly. "Yes. They're on their way right now to get us."

"Can they even get in here?"

Patrick shrugged. "We're about to find out. I guess the road has been salted, so it's just a matter of navigating your driveway, and we've got some big trucks."

"Okay, great. But you ladies go. I should stay here and tend the fire, so to speak. It's not safe to leave the heater unattended, and I still don't want the pipes to freeze. We're not exactly out of the woods yet—"

"You go," Sunny said quickly. Something was going on with her. She wasn't acting like herself. "I'll stay."

"That's nonsense," Harold said. "He's your boyfriend! Besides, it will be nice to have the house to myself for a while." He gave Sunny a look that suggested this didn't happen often. Or at all.

"Your father's right, Sun." Gloria left Patrick to go pull her daughter up off the couch. Sunny resisted but not enough. "Let's go get dressed." She dragged her daughter out of the room like a four-year-old.

Patrick watched them go and then looked at Harold. "Do you have more kerosene? This thing must be about run dry."

"Oh, yes. Don't you worry."

Patrick was worried, though. And not about the kerosene. Something else was going on. He wasn't sure what it was, but his gut told him it wasn't good.

Chapter 21

♥

Sunny was still hiding in her freezing cold bedroom when she heard the rumble of Bannon trucks in her yard. She looked in the mirror. *What am I going to do?* she silently asked herself. She did not want to go to the ranch. As much as she'd love to see Brooke, this was going to be a mess.

She was about to walk directly into the heart of Bannon-land with a Bannon *and* with a mother who was excited about her pretend relationship with said Bannon. How was she going to keep up this ruse? She couldn't. Which meant she had to tell her mother the truth. Which was going to cause a lot of pain and suffering.

This is what happens when you lie, she told herself. *Even if it's a little lie.* She tipped her head back and looked at the ceiling. How had she gotten into this mess?

And more importantly, how was she going to get out of it?

"Sunny!" her mother called from the kitchen. "Come see!"

She rolled her eyes. She'd seen plow trucks before. She didn't need to go gawk at them now. But what else was she going to do, hide in her room until the power came back on?

Till Patrick went back to Africa?

The thought made her sick, but she tried to reason away the sickness: This wasn't a big deal. She had a crush on a handsome cowboy. He had to go home. She would be okay. She'd always been okay. Who she was hadn't changed just because she had a crush.

But it was more than a crush, and she knew it.

No. It didn't have to be.

She swallowed hard, smoothed her hair back, and left her bedroom so she could go pretend to be excited about trucks.

She nearly smashed into Patrick as she stepped out of the room. Oh no, he had his cowboy hat on again. That thing made her thinking cloudy.

He caught her arm. "Hey." The concern in his soft, deep voice was palpable. "Are you okay?"

She nodded quickly and tried to subtly remove her arm from his grasp. This was going to be a lot easier if she stopped letting him touch her.

Her move hadn't been subtle enough not to hurt his feelings. She could see it in his eyes, and that hurt caused a pain in her chest that she could barely tolerate.

He dropped his hand. "What's wrong?"

She shook her head. "Nothing. I promise." Oh great, now she was lying to him too. "I'm sorry. I just ..." She had to come up with something. She couldn't exactly tell him the truth, that she was trying to push him away because he had to go back to Africa. "I just don't think we all need to go back to your ranch."

"No one thinks you *need* to. We invited you so that you can be more comfortable." Now he sounded defensive.

Fine. She would have to be gentler when she pushed him away. "Okay. Thank you."

He stepped aside, so she could go first down the hallway, and she could feel his eyes on her back as she walked. All she wanted to do was turn around, throw her arms around him, bury her head in his chest, and tell him she was sorry. Tell him he was the most magnetic man on the planet.

He opened the door for her and then left her to go talk to the men by his pickup.

Maybe she should come clean. Brutal honesty had always been her M. O., not this pretending to be someone's girlfriend and then pretending not to like him. All the acting was making her dizzy. She watched him interacting with the pack of cowboys who'd come to rescue them. What would happen if she told him everything? She knew he wouldn't reject her outright. He obviously liked her, at least a little. Enough to kiss her.

A thought occurred to her, and her stomach rolled. What if he *really* liked her? What if his feelings were as strong as hers? Was there a possibility that he wouldn't go back to Africa? She didn't think so, but if there was even the slimmest chance, then she couldn't gamble with that.

She couldn't interfere with what he'd chosen to do with his life. She couldn't come between him and his ministry, between him and what he was doing for God.

So whether or not he returned her feelings, she had to nip this in the bud. She would continue to be cold, he would assume she was a big old jerk and that he'd been wrong about her, and he would decide *not* to like her, and then he could head back to Africa with a clean mind.

Yes. That was the plan.

Chapter 22

Patrick opened his truck door and motioned for Sunny to climb in. Gloria came running toward them, and he opened a rear door for her. She lithely floated up into the cab as if she did it every day, and he shut the door behind her. He didn't know how old Gloria was, but she was young at heart. He could see where Sunny got her spirit. As he rounded the truck to his side, he realized how much he was missing that spirit right now.

He got behind the wheel and looked at Sunny, who stared straight ahead. What was going on? She'd turned into an ice princess. Maybe she just wasn't a morning person. He put the truck in drive and started up the slight incline that had done him in the day before.

"They pulled your car out too. It's back at the ranch."

"Oh!" She sounded as if she'd forgotten all about her car. "Thank you."

They rode in silence. This stank. He couldn't exactly have a heart to heart with her mother in the back seat.

"Are you two fighting?"

Point proven. This reminded him of their ruse. He couldn't exactly call ahead and ask Callum to run around telling everyone the lie.

At the stop sign, he pulled out his phone.

"No texting, even at stop signs," Gloria scolded.

"I know, I know. Hang on." He started swiping.

She reached over the seat and slapped at his hand, knocking his phone to the floor. "I said no texting!"

He didn't know whether to be horrified or amused.

Sunny chose the latter. He looked at her. Good, the spark was back in her eyes. For a moment at least.

He started driving again. They would just have to wing this thing. He focused on the road, but his peripheral vision caught the slightest movement beside him. He looked at Sunny without turning his head. Ever so slowly, she was bending over. Her fingers were outstretched, though she still stared straight ahead. What was she up to? Then she saw where her fingers were pointing.

The phone. Of course.

He slowed down to give her more time.

A minute later, she had the phone in her lap.

Good grief, was she adorable.

She was discreetly tucking his phone into her coat pocket when he turned his truck into the ranch's driveway. He could barely stand the suspense, but he waited until they were out of the truck to whisper into her ear. "Who did you text, and what did you say?"

"Wouldn't you like to know?" She smiled playfully but then the smile dropped off her face as if she'd been stuck with a pin. "You didn't have Brooke's number."

He did, but it wasn't labeled yet. "Sorry."

"I should have it memorized, but I don't. Anyway, I texted Callum."

"Oh boy."

"It's okay. He already thinks I'm nuts."

"That's an exaggeration."

She looked around. "You can hardly tell there was a storm here." The driveway and yard had been plowed and sanded, and the snow continued to taper off.

Shane met them in the yard. "Hey there, brother!" His eyes were dancing, as if he had some joke he couldn't wait to share. He looked at Sunny, looked back to Patrick, and then shook his head and laughed.

"Looks like Callum got the word out," Patrick mumbled.

"Got the word out about what?" Gloria asked. Her hearing was stellar.

"Oh, nothing." Patrick motioned for her to go inside. "After you."

She stepped over the threshold and then stopped, blocking the rest of them from entering. "Oh my goodness!" She sounded like she was seeing the Rocky Mountains for the first time. It was a bit much, frankly. Callum's home was nice, but it wasn't the Hearst Castle.

Ma breezed into the foyer. "Welcome! Welcome!"

Gloria looked her up and down, maybe even a little judgmentally. With anyone else, Patrick might have been worried about conflict, but he'd yet to meet a person Ma couldn't win over.

"Come in, come in, have you had your breakfast?"

"I don't eat breakfast," Gloria said sternly. Then her voice grew humbler when she added, "I could sure use some coffee, though."

"Absolutely, come right in."

Unsurprisingly, the table was covered with dishes of food. Warm bread, cheesy scrambled eggs, bacon, and crispy hash browns. His stomach roared to life, but he hesitated. He wanted to see where Sunny would sit. She was pale. Without thinking, he put his hand on the small of her back to comfort her, and she stepped away from his touch.

This hurt. Quite a bit. More than he thought it could. More than he wanted it to. Fine. He would let go of whatever he thought was happening. It obviously wasn't. He'd been wrong.

He sat down. She hesitated and then sat beside him. Gloria went straight to the coffee machine, where Ma was brewing her a cup. Then she sat down across the table from them and stared at them. Patrick felt pressure to play the part. He could come to terms with the fact that Sunny and he weren't going to be a thing, but that didn't mean they had to disappoint Gloria. He didn't want to upset her, especially not now in front of such a large audience. He wasn't sure how she would react to figuring out the truth; she was proving herself to be a tad unpredictable. She was still staring at them, though, and Patrick fought the urge to put his arm around Sunny. Yes, he was acting in a silly play that he himself had decided to produce, but that didn't mean he was going to harass the leading female.

The fact that Gloria could focus on them so intently was impressive because there was a lot going on in the room. First, the food was tempting, but Gloria completely ignored it. Then, the audience grew and grew. School had been canceled, so Callum's boys were there eating like they'd never seen food before. Shane had just shown up, and shortly after, Liam and Blade had strolled in. Blade wore chaps. Patrick found this amusing. Brooke, who was almost as pale as Sunny, had come downstairs to see her friend. And Deedee was there. She was staring at them too. She looked confused.

Callum's boys started fighting over the last strips of bacon.

"No fighting at my table," Ma scolded. "I can make more bacon." She turned from the stove and surveyed the crowded table. "Well, I do like having all my cubs in my den. Too bad Finn isn't here."

"We have Finn all the time," Shane said. "But Patrick's a treat." He was also staring at them now, his eyes dancing with the joke.

Patrick chewed faster. He was suddenly very excited to retire to the living room. Or anywhere less populated. This was his family, but it still felt like a crowd, and the longer he lived in Africa, the less comfortable he was in crowds. Airports were particularly stressful, and his family kept giving him reasons to spend hours in them.

"What's wrong?" Gloria asked loudly.

"Nothing's wrong, Mom," Sunny said quickly. She sounded so uncomfortable that Patrick longed to comfort her.

"Something's wrong." She was staring at him now.

No one said anything.

"Callum, how would you feel about building an indoor arena?" Shane asked in an obvious attempt to steer the conversation in a different direction.

Patrick was grateful for the effort.

"Sure would be nice on a day like today to be able to ride, and I was thinking that Blade here would love to give riding lessons to local kids."

"I would?" Blade's eyes were huge balls of shock.

Shane winked at her.

Callum had looked annoyed by the initial question, but his eyes lit up at the mention of lessons. "You know what, that's not a half bad idea. What do you think, Blade?"

"About riding lessons?" Her tone made it clear what she thought.

"Come on, honey. You'd be great at that," Liam said, and Patrick almost laughed out loud at the sweetness in his tone. Liam was a brand-new man.

She didn't look convinced, though, no matter how sweet his tone was.

"Riding lessons maybe," Callum said, "but I meant about the indoor arena. It might be useful for lots of things."

"Of course it would be," Blade said slowly, as if she didn't really want to mean it.

Callum gave Shane a solemn nod. "Good thinking, brother."

This was interesting. Callum usually liked to be the one who came up with the ideas. Maybe being in love again had softened him.

"What's wrong?" Gloria demanded, raising her voice.

Chapter 23

♥

"Mom, nothing is wrong. Please." Sunny wanted to say more. She wanted to say, "Please don't do this here. Please don't embarrass me. Please don't embarrass yourself." But those words would embarrass them both. She wished her dad were here. He was good at handling her mother.

Sunny hadn't noticed her approach, but Mrs. Bannon was suddenly there, wedging a chair between Gloria and Shane. "So, Brooke tells me you have an art show coming up in Rapid City? Congratulat—"

Gloria slammed the table with both hands, making everything rattle and sloshing Sunny's coffee out of its mug. "Why is no one answering me?" she screeched.

Callum tilted his head toward the doorway, and his boys left the room.

Sunny looked down at her lap. "Mom, I've answered you twice. You're just not listening."

"You're lying to me!" She looked around the room. "Everyone is lying to me!"

Sunny knew then that their simple fib had been dangerous. Her mother was already paranoid and untrusting. Of course she would suspect them. And then she would be hurt when she learned the truth. Their lie would further convince her that she was right to not trust anyone—even her daughter.

Gloria looked at Mrs. Bannon, her eyes wild. "Can't anybody else see that there's something wrong? They were so happy together, and now they can barely look at each other! What happened?"

Patrick leaned forward and put his elbows on the table. "I'm sorry, Gloria."

Please, don't, Sunny silently pleaded. He did not know how to handle her mother. He was going to make things worse.

"Sunny was a bit cranky with me this morning, and I got annoyed. I shouldn't be annoyed. I should be more gracious. I know she didn't get much sleep last night."

Sunny put her hand on his arm. "It's okay." Her voice sounded strained. She looked at her mother. "As I've tried to say a million times, Mom, Patrick and I are not really a couple. Yes, he's wonderful, and yes, I think the world of him, but he has to go back to Africa, so please stop expecting us to act like lovebirds." She stopped for a few seconds, hoping that would sink in. "Don't you agree that it wouldn't be too wise for me to get too attached?"

Sunny couldn't quite read her mother's face, and that worried her.

"You're in love with him! Just go to Africa!"

Oh, perfect. How could she possibly tell her mother that she couldn't leave her alone with her father? That would be so insulting. Her mother would never recover from such a blow.

"I don't want to move to Africa," she said softly.

Her mother stood, sliding the chair back with a clunk. "You're a selfish brat! How dare you let him get away! You're going to be single forever!" She stomped out of the room, which took a while because it was a long way around the table and through the doorway.

Yes. Sunny knew this. She would very likely be single for a very long time. But she hadn't needed that announced in front of the entire Bannon clan. She started to get up, but Mrs. Bannon was already beside her. "Let me, dear. We moms can often speak a language that only we can understand."

Gratefully, Sunny sat down. But she couldn't pick her head up. She couldn't face any of them.

"I'm sorry," Patrick whispered.

She nodded, and against her will, tears slid out of her eyes. "It's okay. I know you didn't mean for anything bad to come of it."

"I should've known better, though. Any amount of dishonesty causes strife." He sighed. "It just seemed so simple."

"It's like lying to a child," Sunny said. She'd done it to her mom a million times. "It seems like the best thing to do, like it will protect them. But it doesn't." Her heart wanted her to look at him, but she couldn't make her eyes do it.

"And I probably shouldn't lie to my kids either, when I have them." He chuckled. "So I guess that means Santa is out."

Shane gasped dramatically. "What do you mean? Santa is a lie?"

Everyone around the table laughed, and this eased her tension and her embarrassment significantly. She took a deep breath and managed to look at Patrick. He was so handsome, but it was more than that. There was a beauty to his spirit that shone through his face, through his smile, through his eyes. She was really going to miss him. She remembered how his lips had felt on hers, even though it had been the briefest of kisses, and she almost burst into tears.

She looked at Callum. "Have you heard anything about when the power might be back on?" She wanted to go home. She needed to get away from Patrick.

He nodded stoically. "But I don't put much stock in it. They were saying ten this morning, but when I recently checked, they'd pushed it back till noon. They could keep pushing it back. But you're welcome to stay here as long as you like." Callum wisely sensed her discomfort. "And don't feel like you have to participate in all the family moments. I certainly don't." He laughed, and Brooke joined him. The sound of her best friend's laughter was a balm to her soul. "So if you need a place to sneak away to, we can make that happen." He looked at Shane. "Too bad we didn't have a nice, big, heated indoor arena for her to go ride around in."

Shane laughed and swept his arm in front of him. "See? That's what I'm saying!"

Sunny mopped up her spilled coffee with her napkin and took a drink of what was left. It was cold. Her food was cold too, but she still wanted to eat it, so she picked up her fork, silently praying for heaven to send electricity.

Chapter 24

Patrick's phone rang. He didn't want to look at it, but he was always worried that his team was calling. This time he was right. He answered in English because he didn't know who exactly was calling, but when Ekow answered with a flurry of words in his own tongue, Patrick switched gears. He got up and excused himself from the table, his heart racing. He must have heard that wrong.

"Slow down, Ekow," he said in Ekow's language. "What happened?"

Ekow did slow down and delivered the same message using the same words. So Patrick hadn't heard wrong the first time. Betsy, his longtime friend and coworker, whom he'd left in charge of his base, had been kidnapped. Patrick's stomach fell out of him. He had to make himself breathe.

Ekow went on to tell him that they were having trouble getting the authorities to help. This was infuriating. Patrick had a good relationship with them. If he were there, he knew he could get them to help.

He had to get back to the mission. He told Ekow to keep him posted. He would get there as fast as he could, but it would probably take him twenty-four hours. Rapid City wasn't exactly a major airport. Neither was the one on the other end of his journey. He hung up and headed back to the kitchen.

Callum looked up at him expectantly.

"Liam," Patrick started, "I am so sorry, but Betsy's been kidnapped."

"Oh no." Deedee looked appropriately horrified.

Patrick nodded.

"Kidnapped by who?" Liam asked. "What can we do?"

"Rebels, probably. I don't know anything yet. They asked for a ransom, but I won't know anything for sure until I can get there and talk to the authorities." He looked at Liam. "I am so sorry. I don't know if I'll be able to get back in time."

Liam waved him away. "Go ahead. Obviously. If you can get back, great. If you can't, we understand." He paused and then waved again. "What are you waiting for? Go!"

"Are there flights going out of Rapid City?" Ma asked. "I'm not sure any planes are taking off right now."

As if he wasn't panicking enough. He hadn't thought of that.

"If they're not, they will be soon," Callum said evenly. "This storm is out of juice. Go ahead and book your flight." He stood up and pushed his chair in. "I'll give you a ride."

"Actually ..." Patrick looked down at Sunny. He didn't want to leave her at all, and definitely not like this, not with how awkward the morning had been. "Would you mind giving me a ride? In one of our trucks?"

Without looking at him, Sunny said, "I'm sorry, I can't leave Mom."

Something in his chest cramped. He'd been so wrong about her. About them. "No worries." He looked at Callum. "Thanks. Let me see when I can fly out."

He stepped out of the kitchen. He didn't want to be around anyone right now. His emotions were going in too many directions—fear, anger, disappointment, hurt, helplessness, more fear—none of them pleasant. He opened his airline app and plugged in the date and locations. Sure enough, he could get a flight this afternoon to Minneapolis, where he would have a monster layover, but he knew from experience he could try to get on standby for other flights that would at least get him on the right continent.

He felt dizzy. Poor Betsy. She was one tough cookie, but she must be so terrified. He silently prayed as he purchased the ticket. Then he went back to the kitchen. "The flight leaves at three, but if you wouldn't mind getting an early start, I'm worried the roads might slow us down."

Callum nodded and stood up. "Sure. Ready to go when you are."

Ma came around the table and wrapped her arms around him. She was crying, and he felt guilty he hadn't noticed. "You keep me posted constantly. Until I hear anything, I will be praying."

He nodded. "Thanks, Ma."

She let go of him and held onto his upper arms. "And if you need anything, and I mean anything, you let us know. We will do whatever we can to get her back."

"I know, Ma." He kissed her on top of the head. Then he started to leave the room again, stopped, thought about speaking to Sunny, and then decided against it.

It didn't take long to pack. He traveled light. Within minutes, he was at the front door.

And then he couldn't leave her.

He set his bag down and went to the kitchen. She didn't look up, so he put a hand on her shoulder. "Could I speak to you for a second?" He half-expected her to say no.

But she didn't say anything. She stood and turned to face him without looking up at him. She too was crying. What did that mean? Despite it all he still wanted to comfort her, so he took her hand and led her into the dim lighting of the hallway. Then he faced her and gently tipped her chin up to hers. "Hey," he said softly. "What is wrong?"

She didn't answer at first. Then, "Your life. It's so crazy. I can't imagine."

Those hadn't been the words he'd expected. "It's usually not this crazy. I promise." *I promise?* Why had he tagged that weird little vow onto the end of his sentence?

Her eyes fell, and he let go of her chin, despite how much he wanted to bring her lips to his. He stepped back a few feet to create some space between them. "I'm sorry I have to run off like this. I didn't want to leave without saying goodbye. I've enjoyed getting to know you."

She nodded without looking up. "Me too," she said with difficulty.

"You may not know this, but I had a huge crush on you in high school." It felt silly talking about high school crushes at a time like this, but he wanted her to know, and he might not get another chance.

She finally looked at him, and her face made it clear that she had not known that. "Really?"

He forced a smile. "Really. So thanks for letting me into your life, even if it was only for a little while." He studied her, but she was a mystery. "I'd like to keep in touch. Maybe I could call you sometime?"

She didn't respond. It seemed she wasn't even breathing.

"Okay then." He leaned forward and kissed her on the top of the head. "Bye, Sunny."

Chapter 25

♥

I t felt like someone had ripped Sunny's heart into pieces. She ducked into the bathroom to get a grip. This was ridiculous. She'd known Patrick forever, but she still didn't know him well enough for it to hurt this bad. What was wrong with her? *Just wait till he leaves*, she told herself. Distance would soothe the hurt. Soon, he would just be a memory, and she would be rolling her eyes at how dramatic she'd been.

She looked at herself in the mirror. Yup. It definitely looked like she'd been crying. She grabbed a hand towel, wet it, and tried to make her eyes less red. This brought some physical relief, but it didn't help her appearance much.

Someone knocked on the door. Really? There had to be a dozen bathrooms in this place, and someone really needed to use this one? "Just a minute."

"Let me in."

Her mother wanted to come into the bathroom with her? That didn't sound like much fun. Sunny opened the door, and her mother looked even wilder than usual. Her eyes were also red, and her hair looked like it belonged on an Einstein poster.

She pushed her way inside, shut the door too loudly, and then locked it—like someone being chased. She turned to face Sunny and leaned on the door.

Sunny really wanted to get out of the bathroom. "What, Mom?"

"What happened?"

"Nothing happened. Will you please stop trying to make drama where there isn't any?"

"I have known you my entire life. And I don't even mean *your* entire life. I mean mine. Since the beginning of time, I have known you, Sunny. You are my daughter. You have always been a part of me."

Her words wore Sunny out, and she had to lean on the sink to keep from sliding to the floor.

"So I know that something happened."

"Really, Mom. Nothing happened. He said goodbye to me. No big deal, you know, because we're *not* an item. We're not anything." It simultaneously hurt and felt freeing to say those words.

"Liar." Her mother stepped closer to her. "Something happened in your heart, Sunny. Tell me about that."

Sunny exhaled forcefully. "You already know, Mom. He's obviously awesome. I obviously have feelings for him. But it doesn't matter because he lives on a different continent, and he's leaving." She looked into her mother's eyes. "Really, it's okay. I'm just a little disappointed." It was so much more than that, and she could see in her mother's eyes that she knew that too.

"You're in love with him."

"Mom, I can't possibly be in love with him. I hardly know him."

"You know him. You've always known him."

She gave her mother a sarcastic look. "Are you about to tell me that I've known him since the beginning of time?"

"Yes," she said, either missing the sarcasm or choosing to ignore it. "I'm starting to think that maybe you have."

Oh for Pete's sake. She didn't need to be listening to her mother's abstract worldviews right now.

"Why don't you just go to Africa?"

She could not answer that question. "First, I don't want to go to Africa. And second, he has not invited me. Because we're not a couple."

Her mother nodded. "But you are."

Sunny sighed. "I'm sorry. I don't know what to tell you. I do like him. But he's leaving, and I'm not moving to Africa. That's insane."

Her mother stepped back. The loving concern on her face had disappeared. It had been replaced by a look of rebuke. "Fine. If you won't be rational, then there's nothing I can do about it."

Sunny would have laughed if she weren't so emotionally exhausted. Rational? Really? Coming from her mother?

"Will you please go after him?" She was pleading now.

"Mom, I can't." And for so many reasons, this was true.

Her mother opened the bathroom door and then looked over her shoulder, not quite looking far enough to see Sunny. "Is it because of me?"

Sunny's breath caught. She couldn't believe she'd asked that question. "I mean ... I don't want to leave my family, of course."

"That's not what I mean, and I think you know it."

Sunny stepped to her and wrapped her arms around her. "Mom, I love you so much. I'm fine. This situation is fine. God will bring me someone who actually lives in South Dakota."

"You didn't answer my question."

Sunny let go of her and stepped back. "You are one reason I don't want to move to Africa, but that is a good thing. Of course I don't want to leave you. You're my mother. I love you."

Chapter 26

♥

Patrick watched the snow-covered rolling hills roll by. This was officially the worst day of his life. Up till now, the day his father died had been the worst. But if something happened to Betsy ...

"Want to talk about it?" Callum asked.

"Not really." Patrick looked out the window. The only one he needed to talk to right now was God. He planned to pray for Betsy's rescue or release until it happened.

"It's not your fault, you know."

Did he mean the Sunny situation or the Betsy situation? "What's not my fault?"

Callum hesitated. "Betsy getting taken. What did you think I meant?"

"Betsy getting taken is absolutely my fault."

He felt Callum's eyes on him. "What?"

He didn't feel like explaining. He closed his eyes and tried to pray.

"You think she got kidnapped because you went home for your brother's wedding?"

Why had Callum bothered to ask him if he wanted to talk about it if he was going to force the conversation either way? "I should have known she wasn't equipped to defend the base."

"You can't be serious." He stopped and waited for Patrick to respond, but he didn't. "And you would have been able to defend it?"

"I would have tried."

"Which means you could well have been killed."

Patrick didn't say anything. He was starting to wish that someone else had given him a ride.

"So maybe you were right where God wanted you to be. Maybe everything will turn out just fine."

"Maybe."

Callum laughed sardonically. "Good ole Patrick. Ever the peacemaker. Always agreeing with me just to shut me up."

Patrick finally looked at him. "Did you want me to argue with you?"

Callum sighed. "No. I don't want anything from you. I'm just trying to help."

"You do help. You help me every day."

"That's just sending money. I want to help in a more personal way."

"Feeding my team is definitely personal." Patrick forced a smile he didn't feel. "But I know what you mean, and you do. Just knowing my family has my back is a huge help."

"And we do. Every second."

"I know that, and I thank you."

Callum reached up and adjusted his hat. "I admire you, brother. I can't imagine living the way you do."

"It's not so bad most of the time."

"Maybe not. But it's not easy. And I didn't even know there were armed rebels running around."

"There often aren't." Patrick realized how tightly his jaw was clenched and tried to relax it. He was going to give himself a headache.

"So what are you going to do when you get there?"

"Talk to the police."

"And they'll help?"

"They should be helping already." Patrick realized he was almost growling and tried to calm his anger.

"Why aren't they?"

"They're understaffed. Underfunded. Undertrained. They're tired. Probably also scared."

"Oh boy."

"Yeah."

"But you can talk them into helping?"

"I think so ... I have to."

Callum was quiet for several minutes, and Patrick was grateful for the break.

"Okay, I don't have any idea what I'm talking about here," Callum started, "so I'm just spit balling ... should we look into hiring some ... I don't even know what to call them. Those private security teams that go international?"

Patrick didn't know what to say. The thought hadn't even occurred to his peacemaker mind. It was crazy. But if it meant getting Betsy back. He puffed out his cheeks and exhaled. "Wow, I hope it doesn't come to that." He looked at Callum. "I wouldn't even know where to begin."

Callum nodded. "I don't either. But if there's one thing I have learned how to do, it's make phone calls."

Patrick nodded. "Okay, then. Thank you."

"You're really fond of Betsy."

"Very. She's been with us for seven years. She's like my right-hand man."

"Is she more than a friend?"

"Good grief, you sound just like Ma. No, she is not. She's old enough to be my mother, and ..."

Callum gave him time to finish his thought. "And what?"

"And I don't have time to date."

"I've noticed."

Patrick didn't take the bait. They were almost to the airport. He just had to hold on a little longer.

"You know ... once you get Betsy back, you could just come home for good."

"I know. But it's not that simple. There are a lot of people there counting on me."

"But don't you think God would send someone else for them to count on?"

"I honestly don't know. I think sometimes God tells people to go and then they don't go."

"Maybe just put out a call? Look for a replacement, hire a replacement, don't leave till he or she is ready."

Patrick gave him some side eye. "Do you miss me? Want me to come home?" Patrick was kidding, but Callum responded with complete seriousness, which was his modus operandi.

"Of course I miss you. But that's not what I'm talking about here."

Patrick was almost afraid to ask. "No?"

"No. I'm talking about how much *you* want to come home."

Patrick tried to dismiss this accusation. "I've always missed home and family, but I also love being there. I have family there too, just a different kind."

"I'm talking about Sunny."

Oh great. "That's nothing."

"She's not nothing."

"I know that." He bristled in her defense. "Of course she's not nothing. I didn't say that at all. She's wonderful. But *we're* not anything. I got snowed into her house. I helped out her family. I—"

"We could have come and got you last night, and you know it."

Patrick didn't know what to say to that. Last night felt like a century ago. "Like I said, she's a nice girl. But I live in Africa." *And she doesn't like me the way I thought she did*, he silently added.

Chapter 27

♥

Mrs. Bannon handed Sunny's mother a fresh cup of coffee. Then she sat down beside her. "So, tell me about your art show."

It was obvious, to Sunny at least, that Patrick's mother was preoccupied. More than that. Worried sick. Yet she was still trying to be a good hostess. What a kind woman.

Gloria shrugged. "Not a big deal. How did you know about it?"

Mrs. Bannon glanced at Sunny. "Your daughter told me."

Her mother looked shocked. "She did?"

"Of course. She's very proud of you."

"She is?"

Sunny was hurt by how stunned her mother looked at this news, but she also looked incredibly happy, and Sunny made a mental note to thank Mrs. Bannon later. She obviously hadn't made it clear to her mother how proud she was of her art. It hadn't felt like something that needed to be said aloud.

That art had been a part of Sunny's life since before she was born. It was a part of who she was. Of course she was proud of her mother. Her mother was an artist.

"I only have a few pieces in it. Nothing like my heyday."

Mrs. Bannon patted her knee. "Well, I'd love to go see it." She looked up at Brooke, who sat beside Sunny clutching a cup of peppermint tea. She'd rubbed so much peppermint oil on her belly that she smelled like a candy cane factory. "Maybe Brooke and I could go together."

Brooke nodded. "Just as long as the show isn't until my second trimester."

Gloria laughed shrilly. "What makes you think you won't be sick in the second trimester?"

"What?" Brooke asked shakily.

"Mom," Sunny tried.

Her mother waved her off. "Oh my goodness, I was sick for ten months with Sunny. I swear my morning sickness started before I was even pregnant."

Brooke looked terrified. Brooke knew Sunny's mother and was usually good about taking her melodrama with a grain of salt, but that didn't appear to be the case this time.

"Mom!" Sunny said with more firmness.

Gloria laughed again and waved her arm around like a scarf in the wind. "Oh, don't worry. It will be worth it!"

"The power is back on here." Shane had just stepped into the living room. Thank God. He looked directly at Sunny. "I'll take a ride out to your house and see if your power is back on? You can come, or I can go on a scouting mission first and report back?"

Sunny popped up. She couldn't wait to get out of there. "We can come. Let's go." She looked back at her mother. "Come on, Mom."

She didn't move.

Great. Now her mother thought Mrs. Bannon was her new best friend, and Sunny was never going to be able to get her out of there.

"Are you sure?" Shane said. "Probably take a while for your house to get warmed back up. I can go check and report back."

One more look at her mother told her she wouldn't be escaping just yet.

Brooke patted the couch cushion beside her. "Come on, Sun. Relax."

Sunny did want to relax. She wanted to take a three-hour nap. Or five. But she didn't want to do it in Patrick's house. She wanted to go somewhere, be alone, and forget about him. But that obviously wasn't going to happen yet, so she sank back down into the plush couch cushions. "Thank you, Shane."

"You bet."

After he left, she looked at her best friend. "I thought he didn't even live here anymore."

"He doesn't, but he works here, and so he's here every day."

"Oh. That's cool. Does he ever sing for you?" She was trying to be funny, but it fell flat.

Brooke chuckled. "No, not since my wedding, but I hear he's headlining Liam's wedding."

"Of course he is." Yet another wedding she wouldn't have a date for. Awesome. She would have to ask him to sprinkle some sad songs in amongst all the joyful ones. Or maybe she should actually try to find a date. The thought made her chest hurt. While actively looking for another man would probably be the best way to forget about Patrick, the thought of it made her feel like she was having a heart attack.

Chapter 28

♥

The Rapid City airport was deserted. Patrick asked the only employee at his airline's counter if there was any way to get to Minneapolis faster. She was polite, but it was clear she thought he was insane. "You could rent a snowmobile?"

He knew she was trying to be funny, but he couldn't muster up a laugh. He was too scared about Betsy. "Can you put me on some list and let me know if something comes up?"

"Sir"—she was done with her joking mood— "the next flight out of here is the one you're booked for, and I highly doubt that one will leave either. I'm sorry."

"No, I'm sorry. I didn't mean to be pushy. It's just an emergency."

Her expression softened. "I'm sorry to hear that."

He rapped his knuckles on the counter and fell away from it. "Thank you for your help."

It never took long to get through Rapid City Airport's security, but this time was probably a record. "Have a nice flight," the woman said as he grabbed his shoes out of the bin.

"Thank you," he said out of habit, but his voice was wooden. Oh well, he would make it up to all these people next time. Betsy would be safe, and he could be as friendly as the old days. It wasn't like this was the last time he would be flying out of Rapid City. A pang shot through him at the thought of missing Liam's wedding. He hoped that wouldn't happen, but he had to make sure his other home was safe and secure before he could leave again.

There was only one other man waiting at his gate, and Patrick chose the seat as far away from him as possible. He faced a wall, closed his eyes, and prayed for Betsy.

Thirty seconds later, he felt someone sit down beside him. He opened his eyes to see the other passenger. Seriously? Patrick could not have made it clearer that he did not want to socialize, and yet someone was sitting so close to him they were touching.

A second glance told him that the man looked a little worse for wear. He was older and sat hunched over. His clothes were shabby, and he needed a shave. His winter hat, pulled down tight over his head, had a large hole in it.

"You look like you could use someone to talk to," the man said.

Patrick sighed. He didn't have time for this. He needed to be praying. But this man, no matter how lacking he was in boundaries, mattered every bit as much to God as Betsy did. "I'm okay. But thank you." He knew he should say more, be kind, be open, but he was struggling.

His phone rang. "Excuse me, sir. Sorry. I have to take this." He half-expected the man to move away, give him some space, but instead he leaned in as if he planned to listen in. Patrick almost laughed.

The caller ID showed him it was the mission. "Hello?"

Ekow answered in his language, speaking excitedly. Patrick's new friend's eyes widened as he realized it wasn't English.

At Ekow's words, breath rushed out of Patrick's lungs, and his entire body relaxed. He'd never felt such relief. "Oh, thank God," he said in Ekow's language.

"Yes, thank God," Ekow repeated.

"And she's okay?"

"I need a translator," the man said. He considered himself very much a part of this moment.

Patrick was too elated to be irritated now, and he smiled at the man. "I'll fill you in in just a second."

Ekow continued to explain what had happened. The local police had tracked Betsy down. The rebels who had taken her were young and foolish and easy to catch. It seemed there were only a few men involved. It wasn't an organized military action. Ekow finished by asking him where he was. When Patrick explained, Ekow said, "Good. Now you can stay home with your family."

A lump formed in Patrick's throat. Could he, though? It was obvious that things weren't safe at the mission. Didn't he have responsibilities there? He didn't respond to Ekow's suggestion. Instead, he thanked him and hung up.

His new friend was staring at him. "Good news?"

Patrick laughed, realized he sounded a little unhinged, and then decided he didn't care. "The best."

He continued to stare.

Patrick exhaled fully. He couldn't remember ever feeling so relieved. Time to get back to being who he was. Crisis mode was over. He offered a hand. "Patrick."

The man shook it. "Isaiah."

Patrick felt his eyebrows go up. "Isaiah? That's a great name."

"Thank you. I come from a long line of Isaiah's. So what was this great news?"

Patrick tried to be concise as he filled him in.

Isaiah was quiet, and Patrick figured he was processing the story. Or he'd lost interest. Either way was fine with Patrick.

Finally, Isaiah said, "And you're in charge of this outfit?"

"Sort of. We are part of a larger agency, but that mission, yes, I'm in charge of it."

"So you have to go back?"

"I do," Patrick said quickly. He had come to terms with it, and it was okay. This was his lot in life. "I live there."

"So why do I sense you don't really want to go?"

Patrick leaned away from the man. He didn't need to be sharing every-thing with some stranger in a deserted airport, no matter how kind the stranger was or how great his name was. This wasn't confession. "It's a long story."

"Aha! So I'm not wrong."

Patrick sighed. "So where are you headed? Why are you sitting in an empty airport during a blizzard?"

He chuckled. "Oh, this isn't a blizzard. Just a dusting."

Patrick managed to not roll his eyes. He knew it was a matter of local pride to act like every storm wasn't as bad as the days of old, but it hadn't been a dusting that had held him captive in Sunny's house. Thinking of her sent a stabbing pain through his chest. The pain surprised him because he hadn't actually ever stopped thinking of her. Even in the height of his panic about Betsy, Sunny had been there in the background, like a backache.

"But to answer your question, my daughter lives in the Twin Cities."

They were waiting for the same flight. And because God had a sense of humor, they were probably going to sit side by side on the plane too—all the way to Minnesota.

"Her husband has just left her, and she's devastated." He sighed. "So I'm going to visit. To do what I can do, which probably isn't much."

"Just caring, just being there ... that will help."

He nodded, staring at the wall. "Her mother passed away a few years ago. She'd be better at this." He shrugged. "But I'm the only parent Sarah has now, so I'm on my way."

"I'm sorry to hear that."

"Me too. But thank you. Now, back to you."

Patrick laughed. "Back to me? There's nothing to get back to. You've heard my story."

"Baloney."

Patrick looked at him in surprise.

"I've heard *part* of your story, and from what I'm gathering, not even the good part."

Patrick chuckled. He pinched the bridge of his nose. He was exhausted. He needed to get on a plane and take a nap.

"I was a medic in Vietnam," Isaiah said after a long silence.

Patrick looked up. "Really? Wow. Thank you for your service."

He nodded solemnly. "I was awarded the Silver Star for my efforts."

This was incredibly humbling. Patrick was at a loss for words.

"I saved the lives of countless men. Ran into battle countless times, carried countless men out of the fire, many of them dead by the time I set them down. But some of them weren't. Some of them lived." He gave Patrick a tired smile. "But you know what the most heroic thing I ever did was?"

Patrick shook his head.

"Raised my daughter."

What?

"You heard me right. I've done some good things in this world, but nothing beats that. My wife and I, we raised a good, strong woman who has raised three good sons. They've done more to make this world a better place than I ever could have imagined."

Patrick wasn't sure what to say. He didn't understand why Isaiah was telling him this. Did he want congratulations? Or did he just want someone to brag to? Maybe he said the same thing to everyone he met.

"Not that those men didn't make the world better. I'm sure they did too. But my daughter, her I know. I can see her contributions to this world. And now she's going through something hard, and she's going to be a powerful testimony to anyone who's watching." Isaiah looked at him. "Who is she?"

"Who is who?"

"Who is the woman you're leaving behind?"

Patrick shifted uncomfortably in his seat. "It's not like that. I barely know her."

"You know her well enough."

Patrick didn't say anything. He stiffly waited for the conversation to end.

"You know her well enough to not want to leave her."

Patrick nodded. "That I do."

"So don't leave her."

Patrick looked at him. What part of this story was Isaiah not understanding? "I have to."

"You only have to do two things in this life, pay taxes and die."

Patrick laughed. He couldn't help it.

"You don't have to leave her."

Patrick sighed. "I do, though. I have responsibilities."

Isaiah held his hands up in the air. "Are you telling me this great big God you serve can't send someone else to do that job? Are you really that special?"

Ouch. "No. But that someone would actually have to go. I've found that not many are willing."

"But some are. Someone will be. But only if you leave so the spot is open for them. Did you ask her to go with you?"

"I did not."

"And why not?"

"Like I said, I barely know her. I can't ask a woman to move to Africa before I ask her on a date."

Isaiah chuckled. "That's an excellent point." He patted Patrick's knee. "I'm just an old man who likes to dole out advice. Makes me feel useful. You can ignore it if you want. How many years have you been doing this?"

"Twelve."

"Might be long enough."

"I don't even think she feels the same way about me."

"Maybe not, but you won't know unless you try."

Patrick was plumb out of arguments.

Isaiah stood and faced him, looking down at him. "And if you're worried that you won't be able to do enough good from wherever you choose to settle down, I assure you, you can love on people anywhere. Unless you actively avoid them, you'll find people to bless."

Chapter 29

♥

Mrs. Bannon's phone rang. She fumbled around looking for it and then found it in one of her many pockets. "Oh! It's Patrick!"

Sunny's breath caught.

Mrs. Bannon hurried to answer.

Sunny strained to hear every word of the conversation while trying to pretend that she wasn't straining. Brooke laid a comforting hand on her knee, and Sunny realized it was bouncing up and down. She forced it to stop.

She couldn't hear Patrick's voice, but the relief on Mrs. Bannon's face told her a lot.

"Oh, thank God." Mrs. Bannon looked up at them. "The police found Betsy. She's fine."

Sunny's mother didn't even blink. She hadn't been particularly invested in Betsy's predicament. Sunny was glad no one was paying any attention to her mother's reaction.

"So does that mean you're coming back?"

The question sent Sunny's spirit leaping, but then Mrs. Bannon's face fell, and just as fast as it had lifted, Sunny's spirit came crashing back down. No, Patrick wasn't coming back. Of course he wasn't. How could either of them have thought that? The situation at the mission obviously wasn't stable if his personnel were getting kidnapped.

Mrs. Bannon told him how much she loved him and then hung up. She opened her mouth to fill them in, but then her phone rang again. "Oh goodness, it's Shane." She answered again.

Mrs. Bannon had six kids. Her phone must ring a lot. And then there were grandkids too. Goodness, the woman was busy. Sunny found herself a little jealous. How fun it would be to have a big family full of people who loved you. She swallowed hard. She might be able to have that someday. Just not today.

Mrs. Bannon hung up again and looked directly at her. "The power is back on at your place too, and Shane helped your father get the furnace going again, but it is very cold in the house." She waved a hand. "No need to be alarmed, but Shane says it's a good thing that the power came back on when it did. Apparently the temperature is dropping even more out there, which is a good thing for the snow, but not so good for reheating a house."

"It's hard to heat anything once the bones are cold," her mother said, somewhat cryptically.

"That's exactly right," Mrs. Bannon agreed, as if her mother had said something perfectly reasonable. "So your dad is on his way here," she said to Sunny before turning to Gloria. "Would you like to help me get some food ready? I'm sure he'd like something warm in his stomach."

Her mother waved a hand. "I'm not really much for cooking, but you go ahead."

Sunny winced, but Mrs. Bannon laughed it off. "Okay then. What does he like to eat?"

As if the question were a particularly tricky one, her mother looked to her for an answer.

Sunny looked up at Mrs. Bannon. "He's not picky. I'm sure he'll eat anything." The canned oysters sprang to mind, and the memory was both sweet and painful. Sunny stood. "I'll help you."

Brooke stood up behind her. "I'll come too. Not to help." She giggled weakly. "But I need more tea."

This left Gloria alone with two teenage boys, but they were both on their phones, so it was sort of like leaving her alone. "You sure you don't want to come, Mom?"

She ignored her.

Sunny took this as a no and followed Mrs. Bannon into the kitchen, which was so full of daylight it was hard to believe they'd just endured a storm. She peeked out the window. "Well, the clouds are definitely breaking."

"They always do," Mrs. Bannon said contemplatively as she opened the fridge. "How does your father feel about bacon?"

"Like the Pope feels about Jesus."

Brooke laughed. "I doubt he's *that* fond of it."

"No really." Sunny turned away from the window. "He is. How can I help?"

Mrs. Bannon started pulling things out of the fridge. "I'm going to make a truly fattening bacon alfredo. So we should balance it with a nice salad. You can be in charge of that if you like. But first you might want to make your dearest friend some more tea."

"No, no," Brooke said quickly. "I'm not that much of an invalid. I can make my own tea." She headed for the cupboards.

Sunny realized that Mrs. Bannon had stopped moving. She was leaning on the counter staring at Sunny. "Wouldn't it be great if you could get married soon and get pregnant? Then you and Brooke could have babies the same age."

Sunny was gobsmacked into silence, but it was obvious that Mrs. Bannon was expecting some sort of response. "Uh ... I'm not sure the timing's going to work out on that."

Mrs. Bannon started moving again and set a giant pot under the faucet. "I wouldn't be so sure."

Brooke turned away from the cupboard and looked at Sunny. "If that's the plan, you'd better hurry up. I'm not sure I'll want to do this again."

"Oh, you will," Mrs. Bannon said quickly. "You'll forget all about the discomfort once your little one is in your arms. And every baby's different. The next one might not give you any trouble at all."

"No?" Brooke said. "Who gave you the most trouble?"

"Callum was a stubborn little thing, but Finn probably takes the cake." She chuckled. "He was in my womb the same time as Deedee, of course, but once I met them, I knew it was Finn who had caused all the ruckus."

Sunny laughed. She'd gone to school with Finn. She had no trouble believing this account.

Mrs. Bannon was looking at her again. "But Patrick. He was one gentle baby. Never gave me a lick of trouble. Such a sweet soul."

Chapter 30

♥

Patrick said goodbye to his mother, hung up the phone, and then called Callum. He filled him in, told him *not* to hire a rescue team, and then hung up again.

He started to call Ekow next, but then he paused. What was he going to say exactly? He'd only just talked to him a few minutes ago. Now he was going to call and say he was just checking in? He took a big breath. He had to get his thoughts in order. Trouble was, they were all tangled up in feelings. *God,* he silently prayed, *give me some wisdom here. I'm feeling a little lost.*

More than a little.

He dialed the mission's number, fully expecting Ekow to answer, but it was Betsy who did. "Betsy!" he cried. "Never been so happy to hear your voice!" He laughed with joy.

"You're lucky you caught me. I'm just about to go to bed."

Of course. He looked at the time. It was a lot later there. "Sorry. I won't keep you. I just wanted to check in. How are you really?"

"I'm really fine. I was quite scared, but there was this odd peace the whole time too. Like I knew that no matter what happened, it would be okay. And they didn't physically hurt me. Just dragged me around a bit."

Patrick shuddered at the image. "I'm glad you had some peace. You had a lot of people praying for you."

"I know. I could feel it."

"So, I know it will probably take some time to process all this, but ..." He wasn't sure how to phrase his question. He didn't want to offend her, and he didn't want to plant ideas, and he didn't want her to feel judged.

"Are you asking me if I'm quitting?"

"Well, I wasn't going to use those words."

"No way," she said, almost before he could finish his sentence. "I'm more determined than ever."

He still struggled to find words. Finally he came up with, "That's great news." Then he decided that what he really wanted to say was, "Thank you."

"You're welcome. Ekow said you're coming home, but you really don't have to. If you want to stay for your brother's wedding, we're fine here."

"Really?"

She laughed. "Of course really. You thought I could handle things before you left. Nothing has changed."

That wasn't exactly true, but he didn't argue. "Can I ask you an unofficial question?"

"Of course. That's my favorite kind."

"Do you think you could handle more things?"

She hesitated before answering. "What more things?"

"Again, off the record, just between us?"

"Goes without saying."

"My job."

He heard her gasp. "Oh."

"Yeah." Then he hurried to add, "I don't know, Betsy. I don't know what I'm doing. I'm just feeling ..."

"Tired?"

It was more than that. "Yes, but ... tired sounds like a negative thing. When I first left to come home, it *was* a negative thing. Now it doesn't quite feel the same. I've had some rest. I'm ready to come back. But ..."

"I get it."

"You do?" He wasn't even getting it.

"Sure. It's not that you don't want to come back. It's that you want to stay home."

"Yeah. Something like that."

"Patrick, you do what you need to do. I can definitely do your job. I've been watching you for years. *Years,* Patrick. You've been doing this a long time. It might be time for a change."

"Thanks, Betsy."

"You're welcome. Stay for the wedding. Pray about it. Think about it. Let me know what you decide. Until then, we're fine here. I promise."

He hung up the phone feeling more at peace than he'd felt in months. Maybe years. Maybe he really could let go. Maybe he really could move on. But was that what God wanted? He started praying again, and when he opened his eyes, the room was brighter. The storm was over. He took out his phone and called Callum again.

"Can you come pick me up?"

"Do you need wise counsel, or do you just need a ride?"

Patrick laughed. "Just a ride."

"Great. I'm tied up here, but I'll send Finn."

"Thanks, Callum."

"You bet, brother. Sit tight."

Patrick stood and stretched. It would be a while till Finn got there, but he still wanted to get closer to the door. He turned, and his eyes met Isaiah's. Unsurprisingly, the man was smiling. Patrick headed his way. "Thank you for your counsel, sir. I'm giving your words a lot of thought."

Isaiah winked. "Good. I'd like to have the plane all to myself." He looked out the window. "If it ever takes off."

Patrick smiled. "It will. You have a nice trip. God bless you." He turned to walk away.

"Patrick?"

He turned back.

"Be a hero, son."

Chapter 31

♥

When Patrick walked into the Bannons' kitchen, Sunny nearly fell out of her chair. What was going on? Hadn't Mrs. Bannon clearly said that he *wasn't* coming back? She couldn't help staring at him.

He gave her a broad smile and looked down at her empty plate. "Are you finished?"

Finished? Finished with what? She followed his eyes to her plate. Oh! The food! "Yes." She jumped up. "Can I get you some?"

Everyone in the room was staring at her.

"No, thank you. Not yet. I was wondering if I could speak to you for a moment." He glanced around the room. "In private."

She nodded and followed him on shaky legs out of the kitchen, down the hallway, and outside, where the yard was bustling with activity. He stopped walking, and she almost ran into him. He leaned on the porch railing, managing to look calm and cool when she felt like she was having a heart attack and running a fever.

"This isn't very private." *Oh Sunny, will you please stop saying stupid things?*

"These guys don't care anything about my personal life." He pointed his chin toward the kitchen window. "But the people in that kitchen?

That's a different story." He moved to the porch swing and then popped up. "Yikes. That's still wet."

Good. She wasn't the only one acting goofy.

He hugged the wall. "Sorry, just trying to stay out of sight of that window."

She looked toward the kitchen and saw Mrs. Bannon watching them. She giggled. At least the woman didn't have binoculars.

"Anyway, I'm sure you've heard about Betsy."

"Yes." She sighed. "Thank God. You must have been so relieved."

"I was. And I was also relieved that I can now hang out here till the wedding."

Till the wedding. Only till the wedding. Then he would have to go back. That was okay. She would take what she could get.

"So, I just have this feeling that time is precious, and I don't really have enough of it to beat around the bush."

"Okay."

"Here's the thing, Sunny. I like you. A lot. You're the most beautiful woman I've ever seen."

His words nearly knocked her back a step.

"But it's more than that. You're funny and kind and you ... you're just *you*. You don't try to be like other people. You're happy to be you."

She didn't know what to say, but his intense gaze suggested it was her turn to talk. "Thank you." It sounded like she'd swallowed a toad. She cleared her throat.

There he was with that giant, dazzling smile again. She opened her mouth to tell him that he was pretty special too, but he started talking again, so she stood there with her mouth open as if she was trying to let the toad out.

"I felt like we had a connection, but then you were kind of ... unconnected." He chuckled. "So I would like to officially ask you out on a date, but if I was wrong about the connection, please let me know and I won't bother you again." He managed to look confused and hopeful at the same time.

She battled with her tongue and then said, "No" too loudly.

His brow furrowed. "No?"

"No, no." *Oh, please just kill me now.* "No, you weren't wrong. Yes, there was a connection. And I'm sorry."

"Sorry for what?"

"For being unconnected."

He stepped closer. "Sorry, that was a stupid word to use. I'm not really very practiced at this."

Good. She didn't want him to be practiced. She wanted to be the only woman he tried to speak lovely words to—ever. "That's okay."

He smiled. "Good." He let out a long breath. "Then, Miss Sunny Bodey, could I take you out on a proper date tomorrow night?"

She nodded. "That would be great."

"Great. I thought maybe we could find a really cold room somewhere and play some Pictionary."

She laughed and then looked up into his twinkling eyes, and the power of them made her stop laughing. "That would be redundant, don't you think?" *Finally, I said something that wasn't completely stupid.*

"Okay, then. How about supper at a nice restaurant?"

She nodded again. "I like nice restaurants."

He laughed. "Good. I do too." And then he pressed his lips to hers.

How was it that she never realized it was going to happen until it was happening? He had ninja lips. They sneaked up on her lips and then were just there, slaying. But his ninja lips lingered longer this time, giving her a chance to participate. She tilted her head to give him better access, and he let out the faintest moan, which gave her great pleasure. This amazing man really *liked* her. How had she gotten so lucky? Who cared that he lived in Africa? At this point, she would wait for him to retire. She could have a long-distance relationship, right? He was worth it. He wrapped his arms around her and pulled her waist into his, and it almost felt like they were melting into each other—two individuals becoming one thing, one new thing that was different and better—

Something that sounded like a bad whistle startled her out of her romantic thoughts, and Patrick broke the kiss and turned his head. She almost grabbed his face and said, "No, no, never mind whatever that was," but she didn't quite dare. She turned to look too, and there stood Blade in the middle of the yard, grinning ear to ear.

"Sorry! Didn't meant to interrupt! Was just trying to cheer you on!" Still grinning, she turned and led her horse toward the stables.

Patrick tilted his head down, resting his forehead on the top of her head. "Sorry," he whispered. "I said the guys out here wouldn't care. I forgot Liam went and hired a woman."

Sunny giggled. "I like her. And I hear she's the best hire Liam's ever done."

Patrick straightened and gazed down into her eyes. "I guess so, since he's going to marry her."

"Not to get ahead of ourselves, but do you have a date for the wedding yet?"

He nodded, and for one crazy second, she suffered disappointment, but then she knew what he was going to say.

"I'm taking you," he whispered, and then he kissed her again.

Chapter 32

♥

Patrick was a bundle of nerves as he pulled into Sunny's parents' driveway. This was silly. He'd spent plenty of time there lately.

Gloria opened the door and snatched the flowers out of his hands. Startled, he didn't have the heart to tell her that those weren't meant for her.

"Come in, come in!" She went to the sink and grabbed a mason jar from the cupboard.

He stepped into the kitchen.

Harold sat at the kitchen table reading a book. "Come on in, friend. Have a seat." He motioned to an empty kitchen chair.

Patrick hadn't really come to hang out with them, but he didn't want to be rude, so he sat. Besides, Sunny was nowhere in sight.

"Sunny!" her mother hollered with a volume so impressive he wondered if she'd startled the horses back at the ranch. Gloria smiled at him. "She'll be right out." How could she possibly know that?

But Sunny *was* right out, wearing a long, flowing dress that looked like a pastel paint pallet. Patrick stood up. "Wow, you look—"

Gloria interrupted his compliment. "Look at the flowers he brought you, Sun!"

Sunny glanced at the mason jar and then looked at him with her big blue eyes. "Thank you, Patrick," she said, her voice soft enough to melt his heart.

"Sit back down, Patrick!" Gloria ordered. "I'll make you some coffee."

"Let them go, Gloria. This is Sunny's date, not ours."

Gloria gave her husband a dirty look.

Sensing there was about to be an argument, Patrick spoke up. "I'll take a rain check on that coffee, though."

Gloria smiled at him sweetly.

"I do love coffee, and it's so nice and warm in this kitchen. Just makes me want to hang out in here."

Harold guffawed and then waved at the door. "You kids get going. Time is of the essence."

Wasn't that the truth. He nodded to Gloria and then put his hand to Sunny's back, stopping just short of touching her. It felt wrong to touch her in front of her father, no matter how innocent his intentions. He opened the door for her, and she grabbed a light coat on her way out. Then she slung it over her shoulder.

"Wow, you sure are acting like it's spring."

She inhaled deeply. "It is. Can't you feel it?"

He couldn't. Not quite. It still felt cold, and he knew they had several weeks of winter left. He thought Liam and Blade were gambling with a May wedding. Snow in May wasn't out of the question. Granted, they were getting married at the church, but they planned on an outdoor reception. He hoped Blade wouldn't have to wear long johns under her gown.

"You seem lost in thought. What are you thinking about?" They had reached the truck, and he opened the door for her.

He definitely didn't want to tell her he was thinking about Blade's long johns. "It's a little weird. I was thinking about Liam's wedding."

"Coming right up." She climbed into the truck.

"Yes, yes, it is." He shut the door and walked around the front of the truck. He was excited for the wedding, but he was also dreading it. He was in a sort of limbo right now, able to enjoy being home without having to make any hard decisions about his future. But soon he would have to make a decision. He climbed into the cab and smiled at her. Good grief, she was beautiful. "Your mom interrupted me, but I was going to tell you that you look gorgeous in that dress."

"Thank you." She looked down at her hands, which were in her lap. She was cute when she was bashful.

"Of course, you'd probably look stunning in a burlap sack too."

She giggled. "I doubt that, but I'd be happy to try sometime. I believe in recycling."

He laughed heartily as he started the truck and turned on the heater. "Feel free to adjust the temperature."

She looked surprised at the offer.

"I'm not a control freak."

She laughed. "Me neither. I can't imagine how stressful that would be, trying to control everything."

"I don't know. But we could ask Callum sometime."

She laughed again. "Stop. That's mean."

He shrugged. "Sorry." He pulled out onto the road, feeling pressure to keep the conversation going. "Are you hungry?"

"Usually. Do you have reservations?"

Oh no. "Do I need them? This is South Dakota!"

She giggled. "No, you don't need them. I was just wondering if you have a plan."

That was a relief. "Good. I know our beloved state has changed a lot since I first went away, but I didn't think it had changed that much."

"Oh I'm sure there are places that do require a reservation, but there's a place right in West Hope that I really like. I was going to suggest it if you didn't have a plan already."

"Sure. Show me the way."

"I will," she said, and she sort of sang the words as if they were lyrics. "And don't say you *went away*. That makes it sound like you went to prison."

He laughed. "No. Haven't been to prison."

"They're talking at church about starting a jail ministry."

Isaiah's words echoed in his mind. *You can love on people anywhere.* "Really? Where do you go to church?"

"Well, my attendance isn't exactly regular, but I've been going to your family's church ever since Brooke and Callum got together."

This made him happy. He would enjoy going to church with Sunny. "I wish I'd been around when they got together. I have trouble picturing it."

"Picturing what?"

"The whole thing. The fighting, and then the softening. I have trouble picturing my brother being romantic."

"From what I hear, he's pretty good at it."

Patrick shook his head. Wonders never ceased.

Chapter 33

♥

"Take this street right here." Sunny pointed out the windshield. She was having doubts. Maybe she shouldn't have suggested a restaurant. Maybe she *was* being a control freak. She hadn't had any big motive for doing so. She just really liked the food here.

Patrick pulled in and shut the engine off. "Looks busy."

"They usually are."

"That's a good sign." He got out of the truck, and she did the same before he could come around and open her door for her. She loved him being all chivalrous, but she didn't need someone to open every door every time.

"Watch your step. That looks icy."

She took that opportunity to grab his arm, which was thick and firm. Digging wells must be hard work. He opened the restaurant door and let her go in first. It was busy, but it seemed a lot of people were there waiting for takeout.

A sign told them to seat themselves, and they found a booth in the corner. It hadn't been bussed yet, but she sat down anyway.

Patrick looked unsure of himself. "I was planning to take you some-where fancier."

"Hey, I'm just excited to get out of the house and to pick what I eat. And not have to do dishes. That *is* fancy."

His expression grew serious. "Oh, I didn't tell you? I am going to order for you."

She raised an eyebrow. "Oh really?"

"Yes. You're having a house salad. No dressing."

"Only if you want to be wearing a salad."

He laughed. "But really. You don't normally get to decide what to eat?"

"Well, I buy my own groceries and eat them when I want to. I'm an adult. But yes, the family meals are usually centered on what Mom likes."

"Like Tuna Helper?"

"Yep."

He was staring at her, and she shifted uncomfortably under his gaze. "You're a good daughter."

"I know."

He laughed.

"And thank you."

A woman arrived with a large tub full of clanking dishes. "Sorry about this."

"You're fine," Sunny said. "It's our fault for picking this table. Don't mean to rush you. I just really wanted a corner seat."

The dishes were collected, and she washed the table with a damp cloth, too busy to talk.

Patrick watched her walk away and then looked at Sunny. "Are you always that friendly with everyone?"

Again, she felt uncomfortable. No one had ever looked at her the way Patrick looked at her, like he was really trying to see her, like he was trying to see all of her, right down to her soul, as if he really wanted to know her.

She shrugged. "Not on purpose. It just comes naturally. I mean, this is South Dakota, after all. Friendliness is sort of the default setting."

"True, but I still think you're pretty good at it. So, you like it here?"

"I wouldn't have suggested it if I didn't."

"No, not the restaurant. I meant West Hope. South Dakota. Do you like living here?"

"Oh." Her mouth got dry all of a sudden. She was slightly embarrassed that she'd misunderstood him, but she also didn't know how to answer his real question.

She was grateful to see a server approaching. They ordered their drinks and picked up their menus, and she thought she was off the hook, but once they'd decided what they were going to order, Patrick asked her again.

"I'm not sure how to answer that," she admitted.

He shrugged. "Well, definitely don't worry about what I'm going to think."

"Oh no. It's not that. It's just ... what *I* think is kind of complicated." She took a deep breath. "I used to *hate* it here. Growing up, I had big dreams of flying the coop. Especially my teen years. I was going to go to college, and I wanted to travel the world. I wanted to get a job that would let me do that. I had a million ideas about that, couldn't quite pick one, but I figured that I would figure that out in college."

"And did you?"

She shook her head and took a sip of her water. She was grateful they'd given her a straw, as her hands were shaking. She carefully set the cup back down. "I took some classes at WDT, but that's as close as I got to college."

He raised his eyebrows. "Last I checked, WDT *is* a college."

"I know, I know, but you know what I mean. It wasn't the college that I planned on."

"What happened? Was it finances?"

He could be nosy, couldn't he? She smiled. "Not really. I would've gotten financial aid, but my mom ... she just got harder and harder, and by the time it was time for me to leave, I just couldn't leave my dad alone with her."

Patrick's eyes grew wide. "Does your dad know that's why you stayed?"

She shrugged. "We've never really discussed it, but he's not stupid."

He leaned back in his seat. "Wow, Sunny. That's a lot."

His gaze was intense, and she dropped her eyes. It was easier to focus on the straw wrapper her fingers were currently twisting and torturing.

Patrick leaned forward and put a hand over hers. "That's quite a sacrifice you made. And continue to make."

She shook her head. "Not really. I mean, it doesn't feel like one. I was disappointed, but not really resentful. And then, the older I've gotten, the less I've despised South Dakota. It has sort of grown on me." She laughed. "I get why people live here now. I used to think it was a waste-land, but it's not. It's a safe, sane place, at least most of the time. People want to raise their children here. I get it."

He pulled his hand away and leaned back again. "She's not in any danger, right? I mean, she's not going to hurt herself."

"Oh, no, no. She's not like that. She's just ..." A memory popped into her head. "I once heard her talking to some artists, and she didn't know I was listening. And it might not have even mattered. Maybe she would have said it in front of me. Anyway, so she's going on and on about how artists are more alive than anyone else. How she feels things so strongly that it hurts, and then all the other artists were just staring at her like they didn't know what she was talking about. I remember being embarrassed, but I'm not now. Now I get it. That's how she exists in the world. She feels things so strongly. That includes things like anger and fear, but it also includes beauty and love." She smiled. "I get her now, and I appreciate her for who she is. *And* she is a talented artist. She never got the attention she wanted and probably deserved, but I think she's very good."

"Did she ever think about moving somewhere with more opportunities? West Hope isn't exactly a hotbed for visual artists."

"Oh, didn't I wish. But no. She said she needed the inspiration here. The plains, the Black Hills, the seasons … she loves it here."

Patrick sighed and looked toward the window. "Yeah. I do too. I'm sure there are other equally miraculous places to live, but I don't think there's any place better."

She shrugged. "I don't know. I hear Paris is pretty cool."

He chuckled. "That's right. You and your Paris."

She grinned.

"What?"

"I like it that you call it *my* Paris."

He laughed. "And *your* catacombs."

Wow, he really did listen to her when she talked. No one else did that. Brooke came close, but only close. "I'm not sure I like that as much. Not sure I want them to be *my* catacombs. That's a little creepy."

He laughed. "Okay. Fair enough. Well, we need to make sure you at least get to visit Paris. Soon."

She didn't know how to respond to that. Was he talking about taking her to Paris? The way he was looking at her, she thought that's exactly what he was saying, and she nearly fainted. A week in Paris with Patrick Bannon? Could life get any better than that?

Chapter 34

♥

Slow down, Patrick told himself. He knew that Sunny liked him, but that didn't mean she wouldn't get freaked out by him offering to whisk her off to Europe. He was thankful when the server came and took their orders.

"You Bannons and your steak," she said when the server had left.

"Hey, go easy on me. I can't defend the steak consumption of others, but I don't get much in West Africa."

"No, I bet not. I'm surprised though that your mother doesn't send you bushels of beef jerky."

He took a drink of his pop and smiled at her. "I wasn't aware they sold beef jerky by the bushel."

She tipped her head back and laughed, as he tried to decide how serious he wanted this conversation to get. He had questions he wanted to ask her, but should they just relax and have fun on their first date? Maybe those questions could wait for date number two. Or seven. But the suspense was killing him.

And she'd sort of opened the door with her talk about traveling. And then he'd slammed it with his weird catacombs joke and then basically offering to fly her to Europe.

"Everything okay?" She was staring at him again. Those blue eyes were so deep, they made it hard to think.

He put his drink down. "Absolutely. I was just thinking."

"About?"

He shrugged. "Everything." *Lame.* "Everything you've said," he clarified. "I really admire what you do for your family, and if you didn't have that responsibility, I would be tempted to invite you to visit me in Africa."

Her jaw dropped. "I would love that. And honestly? My mom isn't an invalid. I think I could get away with a quick visit."

"Not sure how quick it would be. It takes more than twenty-four hours to fly in there, and flights are changed and canceled all the time, so it's taken me as long as three days. And then when you get to the airport, you're still nowhere near the mission. That's another day's travel."

"Sounds awesome." Her eyes suggested she meant that.

"Well, then maybe you could come visit sometime."

She nodded. "I'd love to."

There. Just getting that out in the open made him feel like he had the ball and was crossing the ten-yard line. Might as well go for the touchdown then. "Would it freak you out if I said I was considering quitting the mission?"

She looked only a little less shocked than he expected. He gave her a moment to process what he'd said.

After some time, she said, "Freak out? No, definitely not. But ... are you really thinking about it?" Now she sounded scared.

Oh no. Why hadn't he listened to that inner voice that had told him to slow down?

"I'm sorry." He leaned back. "Forget I said anything. I'm not trying to pressure you."

"Wait, what?"

He was in a pickle now, and he wasn't sure how to get out of it.

"Pressure me into what?"

"I ... didn't mean to freak you out that I was going to smother you."

She laughed, and he was both relieved and a little offended.

"You're not smothering me! Are you kidding?" She cast her eyes as far from him as possible, rubbing her chin on her shoulder. "You said time is precious, right, and that we should be frank with each other?"

Had he said that? Something like that. "Sure."

"Okay. I don't want to suggest that you like me enough to quit the mission, but I admit, when you said you were thinking about it, my first thought was that you were doing it for me, and maybe that's presumptuous and maybe that's arrogant and—"

He stood up, leaned over the table, and silenced her with a kiss, which she sweetly reciprocated.

After he'd sat back down, he took her hand. "I do like you well enough to consider that, but you're not why."

Her face fell.

"At least not entirely. The truth is, I was tired before I ever picked you up in that snowstorm. I was already thinking that maybe I needed a change. I think maybe guilt and obligation would have kept me from acting on that exhaustion for quite some time. Maybe you sped up the process. But I've also had some wise words spoken into my life, and I've been praying about it a lot, and I've come to feel this peace about it." He let out a long breath. "I haven't fully decided yet. I want to give God time to make a course correction if he's going to. But yeah, I'm thinking about not going back. Or rather, about going back for one more visit to say goodbyes and collect my things."

"Can I go with you?" she blurted out.

He almost said, "Sure, we can go for our honeymoon," but he stopped himself just in time. Now that really would freak her out. Besides, he was starting to think they would honeymoon in the catacombs. "Do you have a passport?"

She shook her head.

"You'd better get started on one. They can take a while. And I'll get to work on your visa, just in case."

Chapter 35

♥

When Patrick had told Sunny that Blade and Liam were getting married at the church, Sunny had assumed he meant *in* the church.

That wasn't the case.

Maybe that had been the plan at some point, but it now seemed that it had never been Blade's plan. Sunny sat in the second row of white plastic chairs, and Patrick held her hand in his lap.

The outdoor location wasn't the only thing that surprised Sunny. There were also a zillion people there. Because she could count the people she'd seen Liam talk to on her fingers, she wondered who had invited them all. Then she saw Mrs. Bannon flitting around hugging everyone and figured that maybe Blade and Liam hadn't been fully in charge of the guest list.

Another strange thing was the width of the aisle. "Why are the chairs so far apart?" she asked.

Patrick chuckled. "You'll see."

She looked at him. What did that mean? He didn't expound, so she turned back to watch the crowd. The chairs continued to fill up until she thought maybe the entire town of West Hope was there. Or maybe Blade had brought all of Nebraska.

And then Sunny realized what was going on. The music started, and around the corner came Deedee, dressed in a beautiful yellow gown and sitting on an equally beautiful chestnut.

Sure enough, she rode the horse all the way down the spacious aisle, dismounted, and handed the reins to Holden, the Bannon Ranch's most loyal employee, who stoically led the horse off to the side. Sunny couldn't help but wonder what the horse thought of all this.

Next came Blade's friend Tyra from Nebraska riding a bay. Her dress was identical to Deedee's. Sunny's eyes darted to Deedee, who was now up front adjusting her gown. As Sunny swung her eyes back to the second bridesmaid, she caught sight of Mrs. Bannon in the back, her grin so buoyant Sunny was surprised she wasn't floating.

A trio of violins started to play "The Bridal Chorus," and everyone stood. At first, Sunny had thought the violins were an odd choice, but now that she was listening to them, she was almost swept away by the beauty of it.

And then Blade was on her way, and wasn't she magnificent. Sunny realized then that she'd never really fully trusted Blade to wear a traditional wedding dress. She thought maybe she'd show up in buckskin, but that wasn't the case. She wore an elaborate lacy number with a train that was draped over the back of her horse. She wore a veil, but it wasn't over her face. It fell from a tiara and danced on her bare shoulders.

Chamberlain, to his credit, carried her down the aisle with confidence and poise. He seemed to know the moment was important.

Blade dismounted and exchanged her reins for her bouquet. Sunny stifled a laugh that someone had put Holden in charge of the bride's bouquet. That poor man. He was so often the unsung hero.

Blade shifted her bouquet to one hand and held her other hand out to a woman who sat in the second row. The woman stood, and only then did Sunny see the resemblance. Oh wow! She hadn't known that Blade's mother was coming! How special for both of them. Brooke had told her that Blade had a difficult relationship with her mother and didn't see her often. Sunny's eyes filled with tears. Oh great. She was crying already, and the vows hadn't even started.

Patrick wrapped both his arms around her waist and pulled her back into him as Blade made the rest of the trip down the aisle on her own feet, to where Liam stood waiting, looking about as uncomfortable as she'd ever seen him. But his eyes were locked on his wife-to-be, and he looked riveted.

"Who gives this bride away?" the pastor asked.

Blade's mother gave her hand a squeeze and then let go. "I'm her mother, but the only one in charge of Gwendolyn is Gwendolyn, so I guess she's giving herself away."

A polite chuckle traveled through the crowd, and Liam's face finally broke into a smile.

Blade stepped up in front of him, and he took his hat off and gazed down at her as the crowd took their seats. Sunny slid as close to Patrick as she could. What a perfect day this was. Patrick's fears of an extended winter were unfounded. Spring had sprung. The flowers were popping up, and the birds were chirping. It was the most beautiful wedding she'd been to, better than Brooke's even, though she'd never tell her friend that.

She wondered what a wedding with Patrick might look like but then forced herself to focus on Liam and Blade. This was their day.

Patrick put his arm around her, and Sunny held her breath as Liam and then Blade repeated the vows the pastor recited. They exchanged rings, and Blade said, "You know we're never going to wear these, right?" She smiled up at her man. "Well, I guess we can wear them to church."

The crowd laughed again. They seemed to be loosening up.

When the pastor pronounced them husband and wife, the crowd proved it was loose indeed as everyone started hooting and hollering. At least a dozen people threw cowboy hats into the air, and Sunny looked up to make sure she wasn't going to get hit by one.

When she deemed herself safe, she watched Liam kiss Blade like his life depended on it. Her eyes filled with tears again. She was so, so happy for them.

She realized Patrick's lips were near her ear. A shiver ran through her. "This is nice and all," he said in a soft, deep voice, "but it's a lot."

She looked at him. What was he saying, exactly?

"I don't want my mother to plan our wedding." He whispered so quietly she almost needed subtitles.

Sunny looked at the horses and then at Patrick. "Did your mother plan the horses?"

He hid his laugh with the hand that wasn't around her shoulders. "No, that was all Blade, and you should have heard them arguing about it."

"Is your mother a control freak?" Sunny whispered and instantly felt guilty for saying such a thing.

"Where do you think Callum gets it?"

She too tried to hide her smile. She'd always assumed the Bannon brothers had gotten their traits from their father, whom she'd never known.

"How would you feel about a wedding in Paris?"

Her eyes widened. "Are you proposing to me right now?" The whispered question came out like a rebuke.

He chuckled and then looked front as the pastor invited them all back to the ranch for the reception. He dismissed them, and Patrick practically jumped to his feet. Then he pulled her up out of her chair and into his body. He kissed her long and deep and then pulled away before she was ready. "These last few weeks have been the best weeks of my life."

She wanted to agree, but her tongue wouldn't cooperate.

"And no, you're going to get a proper proposal one day. I was just brainstorming. Thought maybe we could stop in Paris for a few days on the way home from the mission."

"Have you decided, then?"

He nodded. "I've decided." He looked at the spot where his brother and his new sister-in-law had just stood. "I want what they want, and I've prayed and prayed, and God has not told me no. I promise, I've been listening."

"God hasn't told me no either."

Patrick smiled. "Good. Let me make some travel arrangements, and you ... you be on your toes. A proposal is coming."

She stood on those toes and planted her lips on his. When he pulled away, she let her heels touch the ground and rested her head on his chest. "I love you, Patrick Bannon."

"And I love you back, Sunny Bodey."

Chapter 36

♥

Patrick knew that Sunny was freaking out, and he was enjoying it a little. They were packed and ready to leave for Africa the next morning, and he still hadn't proposed. He knew she was wondering what was going on. Every time he dropped something, she'd gasp, and her big, blue eyes would get wide. He'd always feel bad when he'd pick whatever it was up and stand back up without proposing.

They'd gone with Liam and Blade to the Deadwood PBR, and Sunny had held her breath the whole time. The poor thing.

But her suffering was about to stop. He glanced at the sky for the fiftieth time in the last five minutes.

"You seem preoccupied," she said.

"Sorry."

"Don't have to be sorry. Is something wrong?" She bumped her hip into his.

"No. Why would you think something was wrong?

"I don't know. This is the first time you've ever asked me to go for a walk, and now you're ignoring me?"

He laughed. "I'm not ignoring you. I promise. And it's a beautiful day out." He took her hand and swung her arm. "Besides, we won't be able to take another stroll in South Dakota for at least a month."

"Don't say that. I feel bad enough leaving my mother for three weeks. Don't round up to a month."

He chuckled. "Sorry. And don't feel bad. We've got a whole team of people checking in on your parents. They're going to drive her nuts."

"I know." She sighed.

He heard the plane in the distance. Finally. He stopped and located it in the sky. Wow, it was closer than he'd thought. Maybe his hearing was going.

"Besides, aren't we going to go for lots of walks in Africa?"

He smiled. "Yes, we are. And in Paris too."

Her eyes followed his. "Something special about that plane?"

"I think maybe."

It was closing in on them now, and his heart raced. He knew she'd say yes, so why was he so nervous?

"What's it doing?" She sounded more critical than curious, and he almost laughed. It was true that the plane was acting unusual. It turned abruptly and flew in a big loop, which he knew was the beginning of the letter M.

She looked at Patrick. "No, really, what is it doing?"

Patrick tried to act innocent. "What do you mean?"

"What do you mean, what do I mean?" she said, her voice a bit screechy. She sounded a bit like her mother.

This wasn't going as he'd imagined.

"I think something's wrong with it!"

He laughed and pulled her back into his chest. He wrapped his arms around her and whispered, "Shh" into her ear. "Just look."

The plane was on the first R, and he could tell she was still clueless, but when it hit the second R, she gasped.

"Oh, Patrick." She didn't wait for the plane to finish. She spun around and kissed him.

Overflowing with joy, he gently pushed her away. "Look. The show's not over." It almost was, though. As the pilot wrote the M in *me*, his first M was already starting to spread out in the sky. As she stared upward, Patrick reached down and took her hand again. This time, he slid a ring on her finger. She looked down at it and then up at him. "Oh, Patrick," she said again. Then she kissed him.

He pulled away again. "Is that a yes?"

She laughed, kissed him, and then threw her arms around his neck. "Yes, it's a yes. Of course!" He picked her up and spun her around, and her boots kicked out behind her. When he set her back down, she said, "In Paris?"

He nodded. "If you promise not to tell my mother."

She laughed. "She's going to be mad at us."

He shrugged. "Better to ask forgiveness than permission."

She patted him on the chest. "We should do something for the families when we get back."

"We will. We'll have a big shindig. I'll even let Ma plan it. But if it's okay with you, our wedding will be just for us."

She gazed up at him like he was the man of her dreams. "Oh, yes, that is very much okay with me." She kissed him again, and he thought about how excited he was to get back to the mission, so everyone there could meet this amazing woman he could now call his.

Epilogue

♥

F inn Bannon stared up at the sky. *You have got to be kidding me.* He'd known a proposal was coming. Of course he'd known. But he hadn't been expecting it to appear in the *sky*. Good grief, Patrick. Way to make all other proposals look lame. He'd figure that Patrick would propose at the mission or something. But no, Finn hadn't been so lucky.

He dropped his eyes and looked around to make sure no one was around to witness his grumpiness. But it was just him and his horse. Good. The horse wasn't judging him. He looked up at the message again. *Marry me* in looping white cursive letters that were now spreading out into the blue. How had Patrick found someone who could do that? How had Patrick even thought of that? When had his brother become such a romantic?

Finn turned his horse and headed back toward headquarters. He'd had enough work for one day. He wanted to go home and be alone for a while. He realized he was feeling sorry for himself, and he tried to stop it. Yes, he should be happy for Patrick and all his brothers. And of course he was. But now he and Deedee were left single and standing out of the crowd. Granted, they were the youngest, so he could use that as an excuse, but not for long.

He was thirty now. And though he often felt like one, he wasn't a kid anymore. And for the most part, he didn't want to be. He wanted to be a real grownup with a family of his own. But he'd already tried that, and it had ended in disaster. An explosive, embarrassing, painful disaster.

He had failed. He had tried to do the grownup thing. He had tried to love a woman and help raise her children, and she'd thrown that love right back in his face. It had been months, and he could still feel the sting of humiliation.

He dismounted and led the horse into the stable.

"Hey," Blade said. She did a double take. "You okay?"

"Not really. Would you mind taking care of him?" He handed her the reins. "I don't feel so good." This wasn't exactly a lie. He was fine physically, but he still didn't feel good.

"Hey, what's wrong?" She took the reins.

"I'll be fine. Just going to go home and rest."

She grabbed his arm. "Hey, we're family now. You know you can talk to me?" She pretended to crack her knuckles. "If you need me to beat someone up, I'll give it a shot."

He chuckled. "Thanks for making me laugh, but really, I think I just need some sleep."

"All right then. Sleep well. Hope you can make it back for breakfast."

The words stabbed him in the chest. The breakfast. He'd forgotten all about it. "Yeah, I'll probably be here." He had to be. Patrick's sendoff breakfast was a big family event. So he would grin and bear it. But he didn't have to like it. "Have a good afternoon." He didn't hear her answer because he was already out of the stables.

That Blade was a good woman. Liam had done well for himself. So had Callum with Brooke. And Shane with Laurel. And now Patrick with Sunny.

Deedee came running out of the house as he drove by. She waved at him, and he stopped and rolled down the window.

"I didn't even know you were here," he said.

She jumped into the truck uninvited. "I am. Did you hear?"

"I didn't need to. I saw it in the sky."

Deedee groaned. "Let's go get a tub of ice cream and then watch a sad movie."

"In the middle of the afternoon?"

"Yes. In the middle of this gorgeous afternoon. I want to pull the curtains shut and sulk." She looked at him. "Are you going to join me or judge me?"

He chuckled. "Oh no, I'm going to join you. And we're getting hot fudge too."

"Fair enough." She rolled up the window, and the twins rode into town in silence.

Books by Willow White

♥

The Cowboy Billionaire's Enemy
The Cowboy Billionaire's Secret Baby
The Cowboy Billionaire's Ranch Hand
The Cowboy Billionaire's Snowstorm
The Cowboy Billionaire's Best Friend
The Cowgirl Billionaire's Bodyguard